Leaving their hors

little ways up the t
view of the valley.

Being the total geek bookworms they both were, they'd spent their time debating about who created stronger characters, Hemingway or Fitzgerald.

She'd smiled, finding it hard to entirely focus on what he was saying as she gazed into those thoughtful, gold-flecked eyes. He'd caught her looking at him and returned her smile. The way his expression became serious made her think for a moment that he'd wanted to kiss her.

Alarmed, she'd turned away, a decision she had instantly regretted but had later come to appreciate. "I… I'll have to read it again."

He'd cleared his throat, seeming a little embarrassed. "I think I saw it on a shelf back at the house. We should look."

Returning to the present moment, she swallowed a cube of pear practically whole. Now, just like then, his deep hazel eyes pooled with hopefulness, and he looked like the adorable guy who loved great literature as much as she did and had stolen her heart last summer.

Books by Lesley Ann McDaniel

Love Inspired Heartsong Presents

Lights, Cowboy, Action
Big Sky Bachelor
Rocky Mountain Romance

LESLEY ANN McDANIEL

Though she's a Montana girl at heart, Lesley Ann McDaniel now resides in the Seattle area. She juggles a career in theatrical costuming with writing women's and young-adult fiction, along with homeschooling her two daughters. In her spare time she chips away at her goal of reading every book ever written.

LESLEY ANN McDANIEL

Rocky Mountain Romance

If you purchased this book without a cover you should be aware that this book is stolen property. It was reported as "unsold and destroyed" to the publisher, and neither the author nor the publisher has received any payment for this "stripped book."

Recycling programs for this product may not exist in your area.

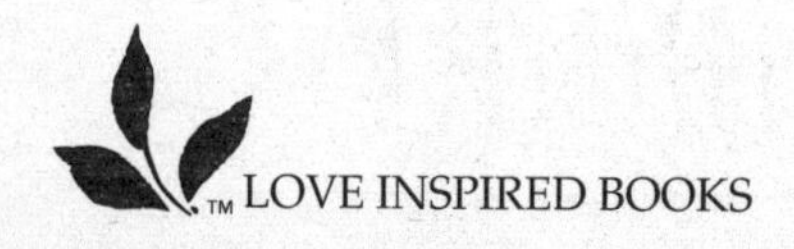

ISBN-13: 978-0-373-48699-1

ROCKY MOUNTAIN ROMANCE

Copyright © 2014 by Lesley Ann McDaniel

All rights reserved. Except for use in any review, the reproduction or utilization of this work in whole or in part in any form by any electronic, mechanical or other means, now known or hereafter invented, including xerography, photocopying and recording, or in any information storage or retrieval system, is forbidden without the written permission of the editorial office, Love Inspired Books, 233 Broadway, New York, NY 10279 U.S.A.

This is a work of fiction. Names, characters, places and incidents are either the product of the author's imagination or are used fictitiously, and any resemblance to actual persons, living or dead, business establishments, events or locales is entirely coincidental.

This edition published by arrangement with Love Inspired Books.

® and TM are trademarks of Love Inspired Books, used under license. Trademarks indicated with ® are registered in the United States Patent and Trademark Office, the Canadian Trade Marks Office and in other countries.

www.Harlequin.com

Printed in U.S.A.

Then said Jesus to those Jews which believed on him, If ye continue in my word, then are ye my disciples indeed; And ye shall know the truth, and the truth shall make you free.

—*John* 8:31–32

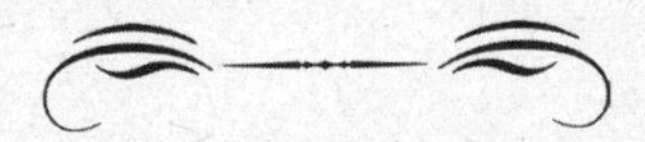

In memory of my dad, Leo Even, whose quiet support has been an ever-present blessing in my life.

Chapter 1

If everything had gone as planned, Sheila Macintosh would have left for the L.A. airport half an hour ago. Instead, she stood in her office, pacifying her frayed nerves with jelly beans and waiting for the printer to spit out the last pages of her design analysis. Why had she allowed herself to cut it this close?

Sheila loved her job as a designer for one of the leading restaurant design firms in Los Angeles, but the responsibility came at a price. She'd put in extra hours for the past month to cover her bases for her upcoming two weeks off. There was nothing like preparing for a vacation to make a girl feel like she needed a vacation.

Tapping her hands on the output tray as if that might actually speed things along, she allowed a fleeting glance through the window at the hazy Hollywood Hills. In just a few short hours, she'd be at the Bar-G Ranch in Thornton Springs, Montana, helping her best friend, Courtney, prepare for the arrival of her first baby. A tingle of anticipation danced across her shoulder blades.

She shuddered. The anticipation, she had to admit, wasn't entirely positive.

Ever since she'd heard Courtney's baby news last summer, a part of her had been secretly resisting this trip. Her last visit to Montana, for Courtney's wedding nearly a year ago, hadn't ended well. Nevertheless, she was determined to keep her senseless anxiety at bay and return to Thornton Springs. That was the least she could do for her dearest friend.

And "senseless" it was. The source of her concern wouldn't even be there this trip. She'd made certain of that. No one else even knew what had happened, so her secret was safe.

Why was she even letting it get to her?

As the final page popped out of the printer, she snapped it up and checked her watch. *Ten o'clock already?* If she hustled to take care of her last little details, she'd still be able to make it to LAX on time. *If* the L.A. traffic cooperated—and that was always a big if.

As she swooped over to her desk, her cell phone buzzed and she gave it a quick glance. *Kevin.* All rational thinking skidded to a halt, colliding with a strange sense of obligation. It was great that he took the time from his workday not only to think of her but also to touch base. But the clock was ticking.

Nervously noting her to-do list, she hit Speaker and started to fit the design pages into a report cover. "Hi, Kevin."

"Hello, beautiful." His voice was like velvet. "Are you at the airport yet?"

"I wish." As pleased as she was to hear from the man she'd been seeing for the past few weeks, she was in too much of a hurry to relax into a conversation. "I haven't even gotten out of the office yet."

"Oh. Really? Well…I suppose you can still make it." The words were thick with the implication that she was being overly optimistic. "You know, it wouldn't hurt my feelings if you decided to postpone your trip."

"Aw, that's sweet, Kevin." She clicked the report cover shut. "But you know Courtney's counting on me."

"Mmm." The noncommittal sound held a subtle edge of pique. "So I can't talk you out of leaving, huh?"

A hint of flirtation in his plea invited her to take her mind off work, which would only compound the problem. She flicked her computer screen out of nap mode. "'Fraid not."

"Fine." He heaved a small sigh. "But don't worry. Two weeks will fly by like you never even left."

Somehow that didn't sound as reassuring as she knew he meant it to. It was her hope that the two weeks would stretch out luxuriously.

She reminded herself to be grateful for Kevin's attentiveness. Her heart had been stomped on more than once by guys who'd started out great and ended up anything but. She'd resolved not to allow that to happen to her again. Kevin seemed to be a true candidate for Mr. Right, and she needed to remind herself not to push him away because of her lingering resentment over a few bad apples.

"Kevin, I really appreciate your call, but I need to get going." Leaning over her keyboard, she pulled up the spreadsheet that corresponded with the design she'd just completed and began typing in some final notes for her assistant. "I promise I'll call when I land in Montana, okay?"

"You'd better." His voice held a touch of playful admonishment. "And text me the address of the place where you're staying. I want to send you something."

"Something for Courtney's baby?" Only half attending to the conversation now, she continued to type.

"Nnno." He drew out the single syllable. "Something for *you*."

His emphasis on the last word both pleased and frightened her. She wasn't ready for any meaningful gifts that might involve making major decisions. "You know you don't have to do that."

"I know. But I want to be sure you're thinking about me."

Words suddenly failed her. Sure, she'd think about him, but his presence in her life was still really new. She didn't expect to keep him at the forefront of her mind while she was away.

Still, she hadn't dated anyone in a long time, and at twenty-seven, her hope of getting married and starting a family was definitely something she should start taking seriously.

Closing the spreadsheet, she picked up her phone and switched it off Speaker as she drew it to her ear. "I'll look forward to seeing you when I get back."

"I'm glad." His voice quivered almost imperceptibly. "Let's plan on going to that new restaurant you've been working on. The one with the aquarium."

She heaved out a sigh. *The Abbott account.* As a restaurant designer, she'd found the elaborate plan for that high-end seafood restaurant to be the toughest she had ever done, and it had been down to the wire getting the analysis completed to the owner's satisfaction before she had to leave town. That had been a major relief.

"Great." She grabbed her linen jacket off the back of her chair. "But you do know the place won't open for at least six months."

He let out a self-assured chortle. "I'm not going anywhere."

Her heart did a little flip. It was a relief to meet someone who wasn't plagued with commitment phobia, as most men in this town seemed to be. Yes, Kevin was a real catch.

A rap at her open office door jolted her, and she looked up to see her assistant, Karl, leaning into the doorway and revving like a racecar. She held up a hand to let him know she'd be right with him.

"I have to run, Kevin."

"Oh. Well…" He paused as if to carefully calculate his words. "Call me when you land. I'll be worried until you do."

The thought of him being "worried" both pleased and disturbed her.

Ending the call, she held up the report she'd just finished. "Karl, I'm glad you're here. Will you give the Roquefort Grill design to Claude for me, please?"

"You can give it to him yourself." He flapped an arm toward the hallway. "He needs to see us both in his office, pronto."

"What? Now?" She slipped her phone into her purse and tugged on her jacket. "But if I'm not out the door in five minutes, I'm in serious danger of missing my flight."

Karl lifted his hands in a "What can I do?" motion and took a few anxious steps backward.

Deflating, she picked up the design and followed him.

In spite of her two-inch open-toe Kate Spade pumps, she managed to match his sprinter-like pace. "Do you know what this is about?"

He took the corner, nearly plowing over a wide-eyed intern. "All I know is he bellowed something about a total redo on the Abbott account and sent me to get you."

"A total redo?" She grabbed his arm, forcing him to stop. "It took us weeks to put that together. I thought Mr. Abbott was ready to sign off on it."

"You know restaurant owners, Sheil." He took the final steps toward the opulent double doors at the end of the hall, pushed one open and gestured for her to precede him. "They don't know what they want."

As they moved into the outer office, a harried administrative assistant wordlessly waved them toward the second set of double doors that led to the inner sanctum of their boss, Claude Maples. Inside, Claude spoke urgently on his phone as he dipped his pointed chin in acknowledgment of their entrance.

Sheila checked her watch. "Three minutes," she mouthed to Karl, who bobbed his shoulders helplessly.

"Macintosh." Claude plunked down his phone. "Abbott wants some changes made." He motioned toward the analysis on his desk—the one she and Karl had slaved over to get to the client on time. "I want you to put everything else on hold and focus solely on this today."

Sheila's eyes flared at Karl, and he backed up a step. Clearly, she was going to get no help from him. "Uh… Mr. Maples…I—"

"This shouldn't be too complicated." Bending over his desk, Claude shuffled through some papers. "He loves the aquarium wall so much that he wants us to bring the under-the-sea effect right into the dining area. I told him you would develop some ideas and we'd have a new analysis to him by tomorrow."

All the air left Sheila's lungs. Short of actually giving the diners scuba suits and plunging them underwater, how was she supposed to bring the effect any more out into the room than it already was? She took a step forward and placed the analysis she'd just finished on his desk next to the other one. "But I'm leaving for the airport right now."

"He has some specific thoughts about ambience and mood that he wants you to incorporate into the concept." Claude continued his paper shuffle. "I trust you can convert his thoughts into something cohesive and rework the design."

She shifted from one foot to the other. Could Claude have a hearing problem she'd never noticed before? "But I can't get it done by tomorrow. I'm leaving town." She glanced at Karl, who seemed to be studying his shoes. She fixed her gaze again on Claude. "You remember. Montana?"

Claude looked up finally, his beady eyes squinting from behind designer frames. "Montana?"

She nodded. He was only in his fifties—far too young to be losing both his hearing *and* his memory. She went on. "My best friend is having a baby?"

"Oh. Yes. Well." His head tipped down again, revealing the start of a bald spot in his otherwise full head of graying hair. "She's not having it *today,* is she?"

"No, I don't think so. But—"

"Fine, then." Turning from the papers, he clicked at his computer. "You have time."

"But she's expecting—"

"Yes, that's what you said." He scowled at the screen.

"No, I mean she's expecting *and* she's expecting me to get there tonight."

"Oh. Well." His focus didn't waver. "You'll work something out."

Sheila felt a migraine coming on. Courtney had made it clear that she wanted Sheila there for the home birth, which could happen at any time if the baby came early. If she postponed her departure, she could easily miss it.

She pulled back her shoulders. "Mr. Maples, you approved my vacation weeks ago."

Frowning at her, he removed his glasses. "And weeks ago, we didn't know that Cameron Abbott would have an eleventh-hour change of heart about his restaurant concept."

"But, sir, I—"

"Macintosh." He narrowed his gaze, pointing his glasses at her like a dart he was aiming to skewer her with. "The Abbott account is the biggest our firm has had in months. If you feel you can't follow through on it, I'll have to turn it over to someone else."

Her heart pounded. She'd worked so hard to blaze a trail for herself in this firm. If she let this account slip from her grasp, it would be like starting from ground zero. She bit her lip so hard it would probably leave a mark.

Claude raised a thick eyebrow. "Is that what you want?"

"No, sir, but I—"

"I didn't think so." He replaced his glasses, then thrust a stack of papers at her. "I've given you a copy of Abbott's requests along with my notes."

Her shoulders drooped as she hoisted the heavy stack and slunk out of the office. Karl caught up to her, clutching the now-defunct analysis in his hands.

"Sorry, Sheil." He sounded genuinely contrite. "I know this trip meant a lot to you."

Meant? Her head swam. If she and Karl pulled an all-nighter, she could still make it out of here by tomorrow.

As they entered her office, anxiety gnawed at her stomach. What was she thinking? Even if they incorporated all the changes by morning, the client would still need to give his approval. They had taken weeks to get this far along. How did she know he wouldn't drag it out for days asking them to tweak the design?

Karl crossed to the coffee bar with the supercharged energy of someone who thrives on completing monumental tasks in an impossibly short time. "Should I make coffee?"

"Coffee. Sure." She spoke absently as she drifted over to her desk chair but didn't sit. A thought wrapped itself around her like a cloak. What if this was a blessing in disguise?

As she absently grabbed a few jelly beans from the bowl on her desk and placed them in her mouth, she watched Karl take a bottle of filtered water from the mini fridge and pour it into the coffeemaker. If she told Courtney she couldn't get away from work after all, then she wouldn't have to risk facing the anguish she'd worked so hard to conceal. Maybe this was what she had secretly been hoping for all along.

As she readjusted her grip on the papers, her eyes lit on the framed photo of her with Courtney at Big Sur the week before Courtney had started working on *North to Montana,* the movie that had taken her to the Treasure State in the first place. She stared solemnly at her BFF, whom she hadn't even seen since Courtney's fairy-tale ranch wedding ten months before. An ache rose in her throat that refused to be swallowed.

Carefully measuring out coffee grounds with a small scoop, Karl spoke over his shoulder. "You want me to cancel your flight?"

Did she? There really wasn't a logical reason for her to avoid Montana. It wasn't the *place* that was the problem, after all, but the memories it held. How could she even consider letting her best friend down just because *she* was a coward?

She dropped the stack of papers onto her desk with a thud. "No. I'm catching my flight. I can do what I need to do on the plane."

Karl whirled around, the coffee scoop in his hand spraying an arc of brown particles on the carpet. "But—"

"It will be fine, Karl." She began shoving papers into her computer bag. "Whatever communicating you and I need to do, we can do over the phone or email."

He charged toward her, still balancing the half-full scoop, as if he'd forgotten he held it. "But Claude said—"

"He said we needed to redo the design. He didn't say I had to stay here to do it."

"But how am I supposed to—"

"You can handle it, Karl." She grabbed her purse and her computer bag.

"But—"

She rounded her desk, meeting him in the middle of the room and putting a hand on his shoulder. "You are perfectly capable of presenting the design to Mr. Abbott without me."

As she moved toward the door, Karl made a little whimpering sound behind her. She stepped into the hallway, giving him one last encouraging look before making a dash for the elevator.

Her stomach tightened painfully. If she didn't love her best friend so much, life right now would be a whole lot simpler.

Sheila watched the lush Montana scenery roll past from inside the vintage Chevy pickup belonging to Courtney's sister-in-law, Janessa. Gazing at those majestic green mountains and the too-blue-to-be-believed late-afternoon sky, she thought how crazy it was that just a few hours ago, she'd been hemmed in by ashen concrete and brown haze.

"Everyone had so much fun at Courtney and Adam's wedding." Janessa had been talking practically nonstop since picking Sheila up at the airport in Helena. "I just hope my wedding is as awesome as my lunkheaded brother's was."

Sheila smiled. At twenty-two, Janessa still had a youthful energy, but she'd grown up a lot since last summer. Not only had she logged almost two semesters of culinary school, but she had opened a successful café and catering business with her best friend, Andra—which Sheila had helped design long-distance—*and* she'd gotten engaged to a former champion bull rider. It had been quite a milestone year for Janessa.

"We're having our reception at Micah's ranch—the one he owns with his dad," Janessa went on. "That's where we're going to live once we're married. We're both teaching horseback riding and junior rodeo there. He has a real heart for kids who wouldn't ordinarily be able to afford activities like that."

Sheila couldn't help a twinge of jealousy at how together Janessa's life seemed compared to her own. Not that she wasn't happy for her. She smiled. "I can't wait to meet Micah."

A look of love spread across Janessa's pretty face. "He's the greatest guy in the world."

The greatest guy in the world. Sheila rolled in her lips. Would she feel that way about Kevin once she got to know him better?

As Janessa turned off the highway and through the fancy gate with the big Bar-G Ranch sign arcing over the top of it, an assemblage of mixed emotions rallied for Sheila's attention. The last time she'd seen these sprawling fields, she'd been heading the other direction, away from the ranch and the total humiliation she'd suffered there. She'd been so angry and hurt that it had taken every ounce of strength she possessed to maintain her composure.

Now, as they neared the house, it all came flooding back as if no time had passed.

What was the matter with her? It wasn't as if she'd be walking back into the same situation. Things would be different now that only a few people would be at the house. This would be a nice peaceful vacation with no upsetting distractions. She'd done everything in her power to make sure of that.

Relaxing a little, she focused on the house, which was surrounded by blossoming trees and colorful spring blooms. She'd fallen in love with this place last summer and excitement brewed at the prospect of staying here again, even though things would be...well...*different.*

As the truck pulled up between the house and the romantic old red barn, the front door swung open and Courtney stepped out onto the colossal front porch. Sheila let out a little shriek.

Ever since Courtney had left L.A. to serve as the personal assistant to Angela Bijou, the star of *North to Montana,* Sheila hadn't gotten to spend much time with her. Courtney had fallen for Adam—the owner of the Bar-G, where they were filming—then had gotten a job assisting Travis Bloom, the A-list movie director who also happened to own a ranch in Thornton Springs. Courtney's life had been unfolding like a story right out of Hollywood ever since.

Biting back her jealousy over yet another friend whose life was totally together, Sheila jumped out of the truck practically before Janessa had brought it to a stop. She bounded up the walkway to where Courtney waited on the top porch step with one hand on the railing and the other on her expanded middle. She looked adorable in maternity jeans and a simple lacy white top.

"You look amazing!" Sheila took the steps two at a time and threw her arms around her best friend.

"And you look like you could use some Big Sky R & R." Courtney took a step back and studied her. "Let's ditch the suit and get you into some vacation duds."

Sheila laughed. They had been through this last summer, so this time she'd come prepared with jeans, T-shirts and a pair of sneakers. Two whole weeks of comfy clothes and flat shoes sounded like paradise to her.

She looked around. "Where are your parents?"

Courtney gave a sardonic chuckle. "My husband is determined to bring out my dad's inner cowboy. They're out riding the range. And my mom is in town shopping for baby things with my mother-in-law."

"You know..." Janessa stood at the bottom of the steps next to a bed of vibrant pink-and-orange petunias. "With all the men around this place, we shouldn't have to carry your bags upstairs." She made a sweeping gesture in the direction of the outlying ranch buildings and the pastures beyond. "Why don't I go rustle up a bellhop before I head back to the café."

"Oh, the *café*." Sheila clapped her hands together at the reminder. Although she'd helped them with the design, she hadn't been able to visit the place in person yet. "I can't wait to see it."

"I know!" Janessa whirled around, her dark brown ponytail swinging to keep up. "I'll be right back with some muscle."

Letting out a small sigh, Courtney watched Janessa round the corner of the house.

"What?" Sheila frowned.

"It's just that we're all a little worried. The café was a huge financial undertaking for those girls. We're praying they can keep it going and pay off the loans they had to take out."

Sheila bit her lower lip. She had done all she could to help the girls prepare, but in the restaurant business, you had to expect the unexpected. "I know they have more things they want to do to the place, and they're going to need to replace their stove soon. Maybe I can give them some ideas when I see it in person."

Courtney's look of concern eased. "There will be plenty of time to go into town later." She grabbed Sheila's arm and pulled her toward the ornately carved front door. "Right now we have some serious catching up to do."

They entered the spacious foyer that was practically the size of the lobby of Sheila's condo building back in L.A. The house, Courtney had told her, hadn't changed much since a past generation of the Greene family had built it in the 1880s. No wonder the movie people had picked it for their Western.

"Come on." Courtney tipped her head toward an

arched doorway that led into the parlor. "You remember Tandy, our ranch cook. She said she'd leave us some fresh lemonade."

Sheila followed her into the warm, inviting room that always made her feel right at home. Maybe it was the soothing colors, a deep sage accented with rich brown velvet drapes, or the nostalgic feel of the high ceilings and tall windows that invoked a simpler era, but Sheila had loved this room from the moment she'd first seen it.

Courtney lowered herself onto one of the brocade settees in front of the dark wood hearth. She reached for a cut-glass pitcher of icy lemonade that sat on a tray in the middle of the coffee table, encircled by matching glasses. She glanced up at Sheila as she started to pour. "I really love your hair!"

"Thanks." Joining her on the settee, Sheila ran her hand through the shaggy almost-to-the-shoulders cut she had adopted just recently. She'd resisted thinking her need to change her hair had anything to do with this trip, but now that she was here, she had to admit to the importance of giving her ego a little pick-me-up just out of principle.

"I figured you wouldn't want to go anywhere tonight," Courtney said. "I thought we could just sit out on the porch and watch the menfolk toss horseshoes or footballs or whatever else they get their hands on."

Sheila gathered her thoughts. There was something she was supposed to do tonight. Oh. Right. *Work.*

"Actually—" she did her best to rustle up a note of nonchalance "—I have a design I need to finish up. It's probably going to take up the whole evening, but after that, I'm all yours."

Courtney frowned. "I thought you were on vacation."

"I am, but you know Claude. He can't live without me."

Courtney's mouth twisted to one side. "Well, he's going to have to. One thing living here has taught me is that there's more to life than work."

Sheila angled her a look. "You still love your job, though. Right?"

"Mr. Bloom is the best boss I've ever had." Courtney smiled. "Oh, that reminds me, I have to update you about *that* situation before Mama Greene gets home." Her face contorted slightly and she rubbed her lower back.

Sheila gave her an assessing look. "How are you feeling?"

"I feel great." Holding out the full glass, Courtney's smile remained on her lips but faded from her eyes.

Sheila narrowed her gaze and took the lemonade. "You don't sound very convincing."

Pouring a second glass, Courtney let out a little sigh. "There's been a slight change in plans, but it's nothing to worry about."

Taking a sip of the deliciously sour liquid, Sheila puckered her face. "What kind of change?"

"Well—" Courtney shrugged "—we've decided not to have the birth at home after all." She took a tiny sip. "My midwife says there's a *small* chance that we might run into some complications, so we decided not to risk it."

"What kind of complications?" Sheila didn't even try to keep the concern out of her voice. This was, after all, her future godson or goddaughter they were talking about.

Courtney raised a reassuring palm. "Nothing for anybody to worry about." She paused. "It's just that we're so far from the hospital out here that if anything did come up…" She batted away the thought with her hand. "I'm so excited to have everyone here in time for the birth."

Sheila slit her eyes. Just as she was about to probe for more details, the sliding doors that led to the opulent Victorian dining room glided open and Janessa bounced in.

"Hey, Sheila, I found you a Sherpa." She waved a presentational arm toward the dining room.

A masculine form appeared in the doorway, causing Sheila to nearly choke on her lemonade. *Ben Jacobs.* She couldn't have been more stunned if a herd of wild Montana horses had suddenly stampeded down the staircase.

Ben stood there looking like a dream. Her worst nightmare. As their eyes met, his tentative smile seemed almost apologetic. He had one thumb hooked in the front pocket of his jeans—which fit him perfectly, she quickly noted—and ran the other hand through his slightly tousled hair in a move that would have been boyishly endearing if she hadn't already caught on to that act.

Her head buzzed and she let out a cough that resembled a horse's whinny as heat scaled her cheeks. At least she could blame the blush on the nearly choking. This was the most awful thing that could have happened. Ben was *not* supposed to be here.

"...can put yourself to good use." The hum in her head turned out to be Courtney talking. "Sheil, you remember my brother, Ben."

Sheila gulped. As if she had a hope in the world of ever forgetting him. Of course, Courtney had no idea of the significant place she'd allowed him to claim in her life. When it had all come crashing down on her, she'd been way too ashamed to tell anyone. If everything went her way, she never would.

Ben took a couple of careful steps into the room and raised an uncertain smile that sent her heartbeat into hyperdrive. Why did he have to be even cuter than she remembered?

"It's really good to see you again." His voice sounded like melted butter. Soft, soothing, delicious.

Her knees went weak, and she was thankful she was already sitting. She had subtly asked Courtney several times who was going to be here for the birth, and never once had the answer included her brother, Ben. When had this plan changed?

"Ben came out from Fresno with Mom and Dad to surprise me," Courtney supplied, as if reading her mind. "Isn't that great?"

Great. Sheila tried but failed to keep her hands from shaking, a fact made all too apparent by the light clinking of the ice in her glass. It had been ten whole months. What was the matter with her?

When she had met Ben the week before Courtney's wedding, she'd been immediately smitten not only by his good looks but by how sweet he was. He shared Courtney's sandy-blond hair and hazel eyes and had a smile that had made her want to follow him around that entire week like a puppy. Now, as she tried to avoid lingering eye contact with him, she felt her pulse kick it up yet another notch. She was hopeless.

Seeing Courtney's puzzled look, she realized she hadn't responded to her question. Not wanting to be rude or appear shell-shocked, she forced herself to look at Ben. "Oh…yes, it's really terrific that you could make it."

Her eyes drifted past Ben just to make sure there

were no more surprise guests—of the female persuasion. There didn't appear to be…not yet, anyway. But a shudder ran up her spine. *That* would be more than her heart could handle.

"Come on, Ben." Janessa waved him toward the foyer. "Her bags are in my truck." She looked at Sheila. "I have to head to work, but let's plan on you coming to the café tomorrow, okay?"

Sheila nodded and managed to utter something along the lines of "Can't wait," as Ben followed Janessa out to the foyer. Courtney started talking again, and the soft creak of the front door let them know when the two of them had gone outside.

"…I'm telling you, romance is in the air around here."

Sheila jumped. "I…I don't—"

"Between my mother-in-law and my boss." Courtney gave her a swat to the arm. "Didn't you hear what I was saying?"

"Oh. Uh…sure." *Right.* Courtney had been updating her on the progress of the relationship between Adam's widowed mother, Elena, and the twice-divorced but now born-again Travis Bloom. "What's up with that?"

"They've been spending a lot of time together. They both swear they're just friends, but I think that's fear talking."

"I can't blame them for wanting to take things slow. I mean, they've both been married before."

"True. But she's been a widow for over a decade, and he's a different man since his first two marriages."

"The born-again bridegroom?" Sheila remembered that Mr. Bloom had made a dramatic turnaround by becoming a Christian later in life, a fact that was now reflected in the movies he made.

"Something like that." Courtney chuckled. "You can just see by the way they look at one another that they're meant to be together. I can *always* tell."

Ugh. Sheila took a big gulp of her drink and decided she'd have to perfect her poker face around her too-perceptive best friend.

The front door creaked again and a moment later Ben appeared, pulling Sheila's suitcase with the laptop bag and her purse hooked over the handle. He gave Courtney a questioning look.

"Blue room, Jeeves," Courtney quipped.

Wordlessly, Ben gave a flicker of what almost looked like hopefulness at Sheila. He lowered his eyes, then headed for the stairs.

"We're putting you in the room you had last summer." Courtney seemed remarkably oblivious to the war being waged in Sheila's heart, thank goodness. "Mama Greene and I figured you and Ben could handle the extra flight of stairs."

Sheila gulped. Last summer she'd stayed on the third floor, but all the rooms had been occupied by wedding guests. The idea of being up there with Ben suddenly felt really intimate. Worse, though, was the thought of there being *someone else* up there, too. She tried not to let her apprehension show. "Just us?"

Courtney gave her a quizzical look.

"I mean…you don't have any other guests…from Adam's side of the family or…*anything?*" She winced inwardly. How dare her shaking voice betray her?

"Nope. Just you two up on the third floor, and my parents on the second."

Well, *that* was a relief, anyway. Courtney went on to say something about dinner and getting settled in, but all Sheila could think about was that if she didn't manage to regain some control of her emotions, she was in for a torturous couple of weeks.

The old feeling was back. The one she'd had no control over last summer and *really* had no control over now. The one that had told her heart to throw caution to the wind and to hope that maybe…maybe…

She snapped to. *Maybe* nothing. This time she was going to listen to her head, not her stupid heart, which had only ever gotten her into trouble. This time she wouldn't fall for Don Juan Jacobs and his smooth lies.

Courtney frowned. "Everything okay?"

She jerked a look at her friend. "Yeah, why?"

"You just got a little quiet." Courtney elbowed her in the ribs.

"Oh. Must be jet lag."

"From one time zone? You *have* gone soft."

Sheila forced a good-humored chuckle. It was too humiliating to confess what an idiot she'd been, especially when it involved her best friend's brother. Besides, Courtney had enough on her mind right now with getting ready for the baby and taking care of last-minute details at her job.

The last thing she needed was to be told that her big brother was a deceitful two-timer.

Chapter 2

The next morning, as Ben walked with his parents along the main street of Thornton Springs, all his senses were on high alert.

He had come to Montana for his sister, of course, and to meet his new little niece or nephew, but the thing that had really lured him away from work and back here was the opportunity to see Sheila again. Her less-than-enthusiastic response to him yesterday had been a painful blow.

He kicked a small rock, sending it skittering off the curb ahead of him. It just didn't make sense. They had hit it off great last summer when they'd both been here for Courtney and Adam's wedding. He'd felt like the proverbial fool for love.

Honestly, it had shocked him when Sheila had acted not only friendly but genuinely interested in him. With her porcelain-smooth skin and beautiful reddish-brown hair, she could easily be a model if she wanted to. But it had been their long conversations about everything from their favorite authors to the latest computer technology that had really snagged his heart.

He had even taken the risk of letting her know he wanted to keep seeing her, even if it had to be long-distance. She had been receptive to the suggestion, but then something had happened. The next day, she had suddenly turned into a pillar of ice. He'd racked his brain trying to figure out what he'd done wrong but had come up empty except for one disturbing thought. Had Sheila turned cold because she had suddenly seen him for the geek he was?

He'd considered asking Courtney if Sheila had said anything to her but had decided against it. It was a little embarrassing admitting he had a thing for his sister's best friend when she was so clearly out of his league.

An uneven breath wheezed from his throat. He should have known it was too good to be true. Guys like him didn't win the hearts of girls like her.

Of course, it didn't help now that she was even prettier than he remembered. She had probably gotten even smarter, too. He closed his eyes as a wave of anxiety worked its way through his gut.

Might as well face it, Ben. You don't stand a chance with her.

His mom clutched his dad by the arm, forcing him to an abrupt halt in front of the movie theater. "Oh, Bob, look. It's the first poster we've seen for Courtney's new movie."

Ben stopped alongside them, but instead of looking at the poster, he scanned the street for the zillionth time. Courtney and Sheila had come into town earlier that morning to work in Courtney's office, and he was well aware that they could run into them at any second.

"What do you think, son?" His dad's voice shifted Ben's attention back to the conversation.

"About…what?"

"Where is your head this morning, dear?" His mom looked at him askance. "We were talking about the movie."

Ben blinked. "What movie?"

"You know. *High Road to Shanghai*." Her look suggested he'd better try a little harder to keep up. "Your sister's movie."

"Oh. Right." He looked at the poster then, which announced that the movie would be opening here in May. No surprise, since its hugely successful director lived just outside of town. "What about it?"

His dad spoke as they started walking again. "I was saying that it looks like a chick flick, and your mother—"

"*I* was saying that if Travis Bloom directed it, it most certainly would not be a 'chick flick.' What do you think, dear?"

He looked up the street to the windows above the ice cream parlor, where Travis Bloom had his offices. Chances were good that Courtney and Sheila were there right now tying up loose ends on this *most-certainly-not-a-chick-flick*. The reminder that they might encounter Sheila twisted the wave of anxiety into a near tsunami.

He winced. "I really don't know, Mom."

From the corner of his eye, he could tell she wore that concerned look she'd so often given him when he was a kid. When he'd refused invitations to join neighborhood softball games in favor of staying inside to play graphical games on Amiga or to mess around with a new thing called the internet. Inwardly, he braced himself for the lecture that was sure to come if he didn't at least pretend to be a little cheerier.

He glanced around for anything to spur a change of subject. "Hey, is anybody hungry? The diner doesn't look too busy." Reaching the corner, he glanced both ways and prepared to cross the street. He sensed his dad wanting to follow his lead, but his mom had rooted herself in place.

"I have a better idea." Her manner made it clear that whatever she was about to say was what they would soon be doing.

Ben exchanged a glance with his dad, who turned to give his full attention to his wife's impending suggestion.

She looked pleased. "Let's have lunch at Janessa's café. We've been waiting to do that for months."

The corners of his dad's mouth turned up in contemplation. "Wonderful idea. Where did the girls say it was?"

Ben's internal tsunami worked its way inland. Courtney had said she and Sheila were going to tour the café at some point today, because Sheila had helped design it. Since it was only just before eleven, the place would probably be between the breakfast rush and the lunch crowd—a logical time for the girls to take a break from work and go over there. The thought caused a bead of sweat to break out on his forehead.

Before he could launch an inner debate over the issue of seeing Sheila versus trying to avoid her, his parents took off across the street. His stomach tightened as he fell into stride behind them.

"They said it was on one of the side streets, dear."

Dad looked around as if he had more than two directions from which to choose.

Mom pointed to the right. "It's around the corner from the Candy Castle, which is right over there."

Rubbing his chin, his dad nodded in agreement and set off resolutely. Ben followed them past a row of old-fashioned brick buildings flanked by colorful awnings and brightly blooming flower boxes. He shoved his fingertips into the back pockets of his jeans and returned to his introspection as he walked. There had to be a reason for Sheila's ice-queen act, but he was way too inexperienced with women to know for sure what it was. He could only guess.

Yes, he was just that pathetic. At twenty-eight, he had barely even dated, much less had anything that might be considered a serious relationship. Small wonder, since his crippling shyness had necessitated a pretty narrow social life. The only places he ever met anybody were work and church, where his options were extremely limited.

The trouble was, the perfect storm of mutual attraction combined with the ability to be himself around a woman never seemed to happen in his world.

Well…that wasn't exactly true—it had happened once. But it had lasted only a week.

Passing by the Candy Castle, he couldn't help but look through the windows. A pain settled in his chest as his eye caught the rows of bins filled with jelly beans. He and Sheila had gone in there daily when they'd been here last summer to stock up on what had turned out to be a mutual favorite. Sadness welled in his throat as he remembered the thrill he'd felt at the discovery that they shared that indulgence in common. He'd go in at some point this week, probably all alone.

He sighed as he followed his parents around the corner, and a big sign with the words *Golden Pear Café* became visible a short distance up the block.

"Why, there it is." His mom clapped her hands, clearly pleased with their ability to navigate in a town no bigger than a postage stamp.

As they forged ahead, Ben tossed around the question that had plagued him for the past ten months. Had Sheila realized what a geek he was, or had her rejection been for some other reason?

They stepped into the café, and he made a quick surveillance sweep with his eyes. The place was fairly busy for this time of day, but he didn't see his sister or Sheila.

The three of them drifted into a short line at the counter composed mostly of people who looked like locals. The cowboy boots and Wrangler jeans were a dead giveaway. Ben gritted his teeth, feeling just slightly out of place in his Big Star Pioncer jeans and gray chambray shirt. It wasn't that he was overdressed or anything; he just wasn't very *cowboy.*

Always a square peg. *Yep.* That was him.

"What looks good to you, Marlene?" Dad put a hand on Mom's back as they studied the menu board, reminding Ben that as far as his parents were concerned, they were actually here to eat, not to act out his little drama called *Desperately Seeking Sheila.*

"Oh, my goodness. It all looks so wonderful. How can I decide?"

"Well, we'll be visiting here for two weeks. I'm sure we'll be coming back to the café more than once. We'll be able to try whatever you want."

Ben gave his dad a crooked smile, knowing how much he loved indulging Mom's enjoyment of food. He swallowed hard. He wanted the opportunity to be a good husband himself to the right woman someday. But he didn't stand a chance of even finding her unless he learned to act like a regular guy.

Like *that* guy. Ben observed a cowboy in front of them talking to Janessa's friend Andra on the other side of the pastry case. Now, this was a real man's man. He was a little taller than Ben and lanky in a Jimmy Stewart sort of way. Not only did he have the wardrobe right, from the worn boots up to the Stetson he held in his hands, but he had the confident attitude. Ben studied him, affecting a little bit of that cowboy stance without being too obvious.

When Andra disappeared through a door that evidently led to the kitchen and his parents stepped up to the counter to order, Ben eased forward. The cowboy turned to tip a nod in acknowledgment as he apparently waited for Andra's return.

Ben cleared his throat. Maybe if he started being a little more outgoing, the habit would grow on him. He took another halting step and spoke to the cowboy. "She seems nice."

The cowboy gave him an amiable look. "How's that?"

"Andra," he clarified. "She seems really nice."

"Yeah." He smiled. "She's been my girl for a little while now." He looked back to where Andra had gone.

"Oh." Ben nodded. "Good choice."

He gave Ben an assessing look. "You're Courtney Greene's brother, aren't you?"

Nodding, Ben stuck out his hand. "I'm Ben Jacobs."

"I remember you from the wedding." The man's face grew even friendlier as he shook Ben's hand with vigor. "I'm Hank. I'm one of the hands over at the Bar-G. Congratulations on becoming an uncle soon."

Ben smiled. He was still a little blown away by that

thought. His kid sister was already married and about to become a mom, a fact that only made him feel more hopeless for his own prospects.

"What are you going to order, Ben?"

Mom waved him over as the teenage girl behind the counter looked at him with a finger poised over her register. He slanted an apologetic smile at Hank and ordered the first item that caught his eye on the board—some kind of steak sandwich.

Just as he finished ordering, the sound of female voices wafted out from the kitchen. Courtney and Janessa appeared, chattering in the way women did when they were excited about something. Panic lodged in his throat. Before he could make a decision between affecting a bravado or running like a coward, out stepped Sheila, and he discovered his third option—freezing like a statue.

When she caught sight of him, her smile dropped and she froze, too. She seemed to be surprised again to see him, but like yesterday, he couldn't tell if that was good or bad.

He gulped. There was something he had to tell her. Something that might change how she felt about him.

Who was he kidding? It probably wouldn't change anything. On the other hand, what did he have to lose? If there was even the slightest chance that the reason for her abrupt change of behavior was the fear of a long-distance relationship, then he had to let her know the computer-programming company he worked for had offered him a transfer to L.A.

He'd come to Montana to find out if he should tell them yes or no.

Standing behind the counter at the Golden Pear, Sheila thought for a second that her heart had actually stopped. Sure, she knew she might run into Ben around the ranch, but seeing him at the café made her consider surreptitiously slipping a cowbell around his neck. At least then she'd have time to either brace herself or run the other way.

Come on, Sheila. She'd better get used to him showing up everywhere for the next couple of weeks. This *was* Thornton Springs, after all, not L.A. All she had to do was avoid being alone with him, and she should survive just fine.

"Hey, Ben." Courtney lobbed him a casual glance. "What are you up to today?"

Sheila winced at the effortless greeting, as if his being here hadn't changed the very configuration of the air in the room.

"I decided to tag along with Mom and Dad." He gestured toward a window table where Mr. and Mrs. Jacobs were settling in.

"Oh, good." Courtney turned to Sheila. "Hey, Sheil. Let's have lunch with my family."

Sheila swallowed so hard it was probably audible, even over the soft Newsboys song wafting from the speaker system. Returning a smile-and-wave from Mr. and Mrs. Jacobs, she sensed Ben's eyes on her, waiting for a response.

A flash of wistfulness for last summer took her by surprise. That had been a heady week, with the two of them as thick as thieves. She had felt so right about spending time with him then. Why couldn't that have been real?

Not wanting to let on that anything was bothering her now, she nodded. Of course she would sit with her best friend's family for lunch. It was no big deal. She didn't even care that Ben was there.

Right.

By the time they'd ordered a couple of pear salads, Ben had moved a second table next to the one his parents occupied and had come back to escort them. This conscientiousness—what she'd taken to be genuine chivalry—had wormed its way into her heart last summer. She gritted her teeth, resolving not to be so easily snowed this time around.

As they reached the table, Courtney took the closest chair. That left two open seats right next to each other. Sheila bit her lip. Of course Courtney would assume she'd want to sit by Ben. As far as she knew, nothing had changed between them. She drew in a breath as he pulled out the chair nearest her, waiting for her to sit.

Why did he have to be such a gentleman?

As she maneuvered around the chair, her eyes met his, catching that glimmer of sincerity she'd once found so appealing. *Ouch.* It stung to not just pick up where they'd left off. She glanced away, certain that if she looked him in the eye for too long, she'd melt like chocolate in a double boiler.

Feeling a wave of heat flush her cheeks, she flipped her hair back from her face. This was crazy. It must have been the small-town air or something, but she was starting to get a little light-headed.

She muttered something that sounded vaguely like "Thank you" and lowered herself into the chair. He took the remaining seat, sitting stiffly with his hands folded on the table.

Normally, she could shed an attraction that was based on false hope, but there was something about Ben that almost made her think she couldn't trust her intuition. *Ridiculous.* He was no different than any of the guys she'd dated in the past who had let her down, often in humiliating ways. She needed to keep him at arm's length or risk making herself vulnerable to his obvious charms.

"Sheila." Mrs. Jacobs regarded the cheerful, high-ceilinged room that had up until recently served as the packing facility for the local candy store. "The café looks just beautiful."

"Thank you." Shifting a little, Sheila attempted to block Ben from her peripheral vision as she looked around proudly at the old-fashioned fishbowl lights, hardwood floors and high stamped-metal ceiling. The intentionally eclectic design made it easy to overlook the mismatched tables and chairs and the floor that needed to be redone.

"Did you notice the display of some of Janessa's rodeo trophies and Andra's culinary awards?" With a presentational sweep of her hand, Sheila pointed out some of the personal touches that adorned the walls of the dining area.

As everyone looked around admiringly, Sheila chewed her lower lip. In spite of her efforts to distract herself, her entire body seemed to vibrate in awareness of Ben's proximity. What was the matter with her, anyway? He was really nothing more than another short-lived crush. Why couldn't she just get over it?

She shifted again, not wanting to appear rude by turning her back on him. She could be polite, but that would be the extent of the attention she'd spare him.

The conversation progressed to how much harder it had been to get the business going than Janessa and Andra had anticipated and the string of unexpected expenses they'd incurred.

"What they really need is to keep the tourists coming in," Courtney explained. "Joe's Diner gets a lot of the day-to-day local business, but the café thrives mostly on catering and out-of-towners."

"It's a good thing the town has gotten so much attention recently." Mrs. Jacobs patted Courtney's hand, as though she considered Thornton Springs' success to be Courtney's own personal doing. "What with your movie being shot here and then Micah competing in your rodeo."

Ben turned his head toward Sheila, as if he wanted to say something just to her. A wisp of warm breath tickled her cheek, and she quickly twisted the other way. Where was Tawny with their drinks? She could sure use a gulp of icy-cold liquid right about now.

When she faced front again, Ben had apparently changed his mind about talking to her. An odd mixture of disappointment and relief coursed through her. Did that even make sense?

"Our Sheila does more than design restaurants—she knows them inside and out." Mr. Jacobs spoke with the optimistic pride of a dad even though he wasn't *her* dad. "Maybe she can give them a few pointers while she's here."

"I'll do whatever I can to help." Her voice felt weak, as if the crazy resistance she had waged against Ben's manly appeal was draining her not only physically and emotionally but vocally, as well.

"Don't forget you're on vacation, Sheil." Courtney's slightly rounded features grew stern. "You already worked all last night. I want you to have some fun while you're here."

"I *am* having fun." Sheila tossed Courtney a playfully defensive glance.

"You know what you should do?" Courtney flicked a finger from Sheila to Ben. "You two should go horseback riding again. Micah would probably take you out this afternoon."

The suggestion kicked Sheila's heart like an angry mule. The last thing she needed right now was to be coerced into spending time with Ben, especially on some secluded horse trail.

Courtney scrunched up her eyes, and Sheila realized that neither she nor Ben had responded.

"I would, but—" Sheila floundered "—you said you needed help with the baby's room."

"True, but you're supposed to be relaxing, too. Besides, I'm sure Ben doesn't want to be stuck painting walls and putting together the crib in all his free time. Right, Ben?"

Sheila cautioned him a glance. He met her eyes, then looked down at his hands. "I'd really like to go riding again. It was fun."

"There, see?" Satisfaction tinged Courtney's tone as if she'd won a round in some battle that only she knew about. "If Ben goes, you have to go. You're better at it than he is."

The comment lit the fuse of a fireworks display in Sheila's chest. Everyone looked at her as if her agreement were imminent and actually a good idea. How was she supposed to get out of this?

Fortunately, the beeping of her phone cut short an almost lie about her recently discovered allergy to horsehair. She quickly pulled the device from her purse and muted the beep, wincing at the sight of Karl's name lighting up the screen. She checked her watch. He was set to do the presentation for Claude and Mr. Abbott in about half an hour. Why was he calling? They had finalized all the details last night, and she had already talked to him once this morning to reassure him.

She scraped back her chair and stood. "Would you excuse me for a minute?" Heading for the door, she clicked Accept on the phone. "What's up?"

"What if he doesn't like it?" He launched straight into a high-pitched lament.

"Karl, we've been over this." She slipped outside so as not to disturb any café patrons. "All you have to do is take notes and ask him leading questions. You've seen me do it a hundred times."

"Yes, but—"

"You're going to do great." She hoped she sounded convincing, but his insecurity made her consider the feasibility of hiring a private jet to get her back to L.A. in time to just do the presentation herself. "We've done exactly what he wanted, and the worst that can happen is he'll ask for more changes. It's going to be fine."

Pacing a few steps toward the curb, she glanced over at the ice cream store on the other side of the main street. The door next to it—which led to the upstairs offices where Courtney worked—opened, and a distinguished-looking middle-aged man with salt-and-pepper hair and a neatly trimmed beard stepped out onto the sidewalk. Sheila took in a breath. Even with his phone to his ear, Travis Bloom looked remarkably laid-back for a big-time movie director with a blockbuster opening in a month.

Karl prattled on, but she was too preoccupied to listen as she watched Mr. Bloom cross the street. Living in L.A., she'd grown used to seeing movie people and was seldom impressed. But Mr. Bloom was different. She had met him at Courtney's wedding and still felt a little wowed in his presence.

Her phone beeped with a second incoming call. She

checked quickly, allowing Karl's voice to grow dim for a second. *Kevin.*

Ugh. Guilt kicked her in the stomach. She'd had a brief conversation with him when her plane landed yesterday. But what with staying up half the night to finish the project and getting up early to go with Courtney to her office, she had completely forgotten her promise to touch base with him again this morning.

"Karl, I have to take this other call. Email me after your meeting, okay?" She barely gave him time to object before clicking over. "Hi, Kevin."

"I didn't wake you, did I?"

The question puzzled her. "Well, no. It's after eleven."

"Right. I just figured you must have slept in. I couldn't think of another reason why you wouldn't have called me this morning."

"Sorry." She rested her elbow in her hand and turned to absentmindedly look through the window into the café. "It's just that—" Ben sat there stirring a glass of soda with a straw "—I've been really busy, and—"

"No worries." The hint of reprimand lifted from Kevin's tone.

Her focus homed in on Ben. No wonder she'd been so easily fooled by him last year. He really did come across as a totally sweet guy. Shy, even. She had to cut herself a break for not seeing him for what he really—

"I really miss you, Sheila."

"Mmm?" His comment jarred her eyes off Ben. "Oh. You, too."

"So I was thinking this time apart would be a great test for us."

"A test?" Her gaze drifted back to the window. If she

didn't know better, she would think Ben was downright innocent. Good thing she knew better.

Ben looked at the chair she'd vacated, then turned his head toward the window where she stood gawking at him. Mortified, she whipped around just as Travis Bloom crossed behind her and reached for the handle of the door next to her.

"Whoa." He fumbled back a step as he held his hands up in mock defense.

Heat raced to her cheeks. She mouthed, "Sorry," relieved as he gave her a warm smile and entered the café.

"…either 'out of sight, out of mind' or 'absence makes the heart grow fonder.'"

"What? Oh. Right." Furtively, she peered through the window again as Mr. Bloom crossed to the table where the Jacobs family sat. They all looked up in welcome.

"So I was thinking I'd like to take our relationship to the next level."

"Next level?"

Speaking to Courtney and her family, Mr. Bloom gesticulated as if he were pitching a movie idea to a bunch of Hollywood bigwigs. They gazed at him with rapt attention. What was going on?

"Yes. I think you and I should be exclusive, don't you?"

"Uh-huh."

Tawny, their head server, who had an orange streak in her black hair and a flair for the dramatic, arrived at the table with their food, and Mr. Bloom said something to her. She nodded animatedly as she delivered the plates and hurried back to the counter.

"Sheila? Don't you?"

"Huh? Oh. Sure."

Tawny said something to Andra's hunky cowboy

boyfriend, Hank, then darted back to the kitchen. Hank sauntered over to the table and joined in what had become a lively discussion.

"Good. Let's celebrate when you get back."

"Sounds good." She watched as other customers twisted in their seats to face Mr. Bloom. "Look, I really should go. Our lunch just arrived."

"Right." Kevin's tone flattened. "Well, call me tonight."

"Will do." She reached for the door as she said goodbye and clicked off, then moved briskly back to the table. "What's going on?"

Courtney spoke up. "Mr. Bloom says he has some big news for the café."

"Oh?" She retook her seat next to Ben, who had stood when she'd arrived and now sat again himself. *Good grief.* Why did she have to find that so endearing?

Janessa and Andra approached the table, with Tawny and a couple of counter workers trailing behind them. Sheila looked over to see the kitchen staff peering out of the pass-through window. Whatever this was, it sure had everyone's interest.

"What is it, Mr. B?" Janessa put her hands in the pockets of her Golden Pear apron.

A sly smile played on his lips as he waited for a hush to fall over the room. "Janessa, Andra..." He held up his hands as if to paint a picture in the air. "How would you like to appear on *Food Fight?*"

Tawny let out a little shriek and put her hands over her mouth.

"You mean—" Andra exchanged a tentative glance with Janessa "—the reality show?"

Sheila held her breath as an expectant silence hovered over the room. This was an incredible opportunity.

Mr. Jacobs leaned forward over his sandwich. "Is that the show where a bunch of famous food people eat in different restaurants and judge which one is best?"

"Yes, dear." Mrs. Jacobs patted her husband's arm. "The one with the clever host. What's his name? Brant? Bradley?"

"Brian Leary!" Tawny looked ready to burst. "I'm such a fan."

"It's a really entertaining show." Sheila liked the idea and hoped to sound supportive. "The judges visit two different restaurants in different cities and determine which is superior."

"Then the winner gets money," Tawny chimed in. "It's totally cool."

"But—" Janessa wrinkled her brow "—how can we possibly be on the show if we haven't applied?"

Mr. Bloom held up a hand. "I got a panicked call last night from my friend Blair, who produces the show. Apparently, one of the places they were set to tape this week had a health-code violation, and they need a last-minute replacement. Blair asked about restaurants in Thornton Springs. Knowing how much publicity the places that compete on this show get, I naturally thought of the Golden Pear."

Andra wrapped her arms around her middle. "I don't know..."

Janessa snapped her a look. "Andra, do you know what this would mean for our business? People actually plan their vacations around the restaurants that win on this show."

"They call them *Food Fight* Road Trips," Tawny added. "I follow their blog."

Janessa's eyes turned pleading. "This could make our little café famous."

"But it's a brutal competition." Andra had a pinched look on her normally restrained face. "Don't restaurants sometimes get trounced on that show?"

"Maybe..." Janessa chimed in. "But the one that gets the best score wins ten thousand dollars. Think about what we could do with that money. We could finish all our plans for this place and have a little cushion in our account."

Andra cocked her head in consideration.

"Not to mention," Sheila added, "the business it would bring to your café."

There was a sense of collective breath-holding in the room as all eyes zeroed in on Andra.

Andra lowered her lids for a moment. When she opened them, she looked upward and gave a resigned nod. "Okay. But I hope we don't regret this."

The room erupted in animated conversation.

"It's just a little reality show," Andra shouted to be heard. "Nothing to get all worked up about." She flicked her hands at her employees, who took their cue to return to their battle stations.

"Well." Mr. Bloom seemed pleased. "Now that that's taken care of, I'll be getting back to work." He looked down at Courtney. "Will I see you in the office this afternoon?"

"Sheila and I will be back in right after lunch." Courtney turned her gaze on Sheila. "Unless she decides to go horseback riding."

A lump rose in Sheila's throat. She'd hoped that subject had been forgotten.

"Fine." Mr. Bloom nodded to the rest of the table and made his exit.

"Well." Mr. Jacobs flashed a grin as he picked up

his fork. "All this excitement has sure worked up my appetite."

As Courtney engaged in conversation with her parents about the baby's room, Sheila dug into her salad. She couldn't help but notice that Ben had a firm two-handed hold on his sandwich but hadn't actually bitten into it. He cleared his throat, then turned his head and leaned toward her slightly. "So..."

Her stomach jumped. *Keep cool, Sheila.* Taking a too-big bite, she angled her head with what she hoped was an attentive but not-too-receptive expression.

"Horseback riding sure sounds like fun." He dipped his chin. "You want to go?"

A hunk of lettuce nearly wedged in her throat as a memory seeped out of the deep place where she'd stuffed it. The two of them up on the beautiful ridge where they'd ridden last year. Leaving their horses with Janessa, they'd walked a little ways up the trail to get a better view of the valley. Being the total geek bookworms they both were, they'd spent their time debating about who created stronger characters, Hemingway or Fitzgerald.

"Jake Barnes or Jay Gatsby," Ben had said, sweeping a hand toward a dead tree that had fallen in the perfect spot to create VIP seating for the view in front of them. "Which one do you find more believable?"

She'd sat pondering the comparison. "I haven't read *The Great Gatsby* since high school, but I remember *The Sun Also Rises* from college. I vote for Ernest. He was a master."

"True, but look at how Fitzgerald wrote Gatsby to seem to be something he isn't. He's really just a poor guy who's trying to convince the woman he loves that he's worthy of her. Brilliantly written."

She'd smiled, finding it hard to entirely focus on what he was saying as she gazed into those thoughtful gold-flecked eyes. He'd caught her looking at him and returned her smile. The way his expression had become serious had made her think for a moment that he'd wanted to kiss her.

Alarmed, she'd turned away, a decision she had instantly regretted but had later come to appreciate. "I… I'll have to read it again."

He'd cleared his throat, seeming a little embarrassed. "I think I saw it on a shelf back at the house. We should look."

Returning to the present moment, she swallowed a cube of pear practically whole. Now, just like then, his deep hazel eyes pooled with hopefulness, and he looked like the adorable guy who loved great literature as much as she did and had stolen her heart last summer.

Her mind raced. What were they talking about? Something about horseback riding. *Right.* He had asked her if she wanted to go with him again and was waiting for her response. Dizziness threatened, and her head started to slowly nod without her full consent.

"Right, Sheil?"

Courtney's voice pierced through her reverie just as she was about to buy a one-way ticket to Ben Fantasyland.

She coughed. "I'm sorry…what?"

Courtney let out a little breath, clearly not thrilled at having to repeat herself. "I was telling my parents about that restaurant design you did. The one with all the fish." Courtney pronged a bite of her salad. "Was that what your assistant was calling about?"

"What…?" Sheila's brain felt blurry, knowing that Ben's question still hung between them unanswered.

Courtney's brow creased. "Wasn't that who called you earlier?"

"Right. Karl." And someone else.... *Kevin.* She narrowed her eyes. What had Kevin said that seemed so important?

Suddenly, it hit her. Kevin had said something about wanting to be "exclusive." And she'd been so distracted she had practically ignored him. What was she thinking? She would be the biggest idiot on earth if she ruined a genuinely promising new relationship just because of a guy like Ben. She pursed her lips. She had almost allowed him to lure her in again, but it wasn't going to work.

Horseback riding. *As if.* She balled up her fist under the table as a snide question played on her lips. *Does* Stephanie *like horseback riding?*

She bit back a surge of irritation and hurt feelings. "I can't go riding." Forcing a small smile, she tilted her head toward Courtney. "We have too much work to do."

"Oh." The disappointment in his voice would have been heartbreaking if she'd bought his nice-guy act. "Maybe later...?"

She stabbed at a disc of cucumber on her plate, ignoring his last words and vowing not to be fooled by him again. Last summer, he'd led her to believe he was interested in her. She had thought she wanted to know everything about him, until she'd found out the one fact that had changed everything.

Just after she'd been lured into agreeing that they should keep seeing each other even if it had to be long-distance, she'd found out that he'd committed a sin of omission.

He'd neglected to tell her that he already had a girlfriend.

Chapter 3

Watching his dad hoist himself onto a horse for the ride he was about to take with Micah, Ben breathed in the earthy scent of the barnyard and rubbed the back of his neck. He had really wanted to go riding, too, but when Sheila had turned down his invitation, the activity had lost its appeal.

Now all he wanted to do was kick himself. Why had he ever thought this trip was a good idea? He should have planned to come out after his niece or nephew was born and after Sheila had gone back home. Too bad it was too late to change his plan.

The worst part of the whole mess was that it didn't seem to matter how cold she was to him. He still liked her. Could his self-esteem really be that low? Yes, apparently, it could.

"I still wish you were going with your father, sweetheart." Standing next to him, his mom gave him the worried look he'd grown so used to over his years of voluntary nonparticipation in most physical activities and social events.

"If the boy says he'd rather stay put, Marlene, let him be. He's just fine."

Good ol' Dad. Ben smiled. Forever coming to his defense.

Mom's look of concern only grew, the way it always did. "I just think a little time outdoors would do him good."

"Marlene, look at the boy." Manipulating the reins to keep control of his horse, Dad waved a hand in Ben's direction. "He *is* outdoors. He'll be fine."

With a pitying shake of her gray-flecked head, his mom gave a resigned sigh. She wouldn't stop cosseting him until he found a wife to take over the job, which meant she might never be relieved of that duty.

As Micah mounted his horse, he tossed Ben a sympathetic look. "We won't go out of cell range, in case there's any news about Courtney."

Ben nodded, tapping the phone in his pocket. "No worries. Have fun."

Watching the horses move slowly out of the corral, Ben admired Micah's way of carrying himself. Of course a guy like him had found a terrific girl to marry. If only Ben could have that kind of self-confidence. As it was, he could barely even open his mouth to talk to a girl. He might as well face it. He was doomed to a life of nothing but long days in front of his computer and long nights in front of his TV. He was the epitome of pathetic.

"Come on, sweetheart." His mom put an arm around his shoulders. "If Tandy will let me into her kitchen, I can bake you some chocolate chip cookies. They're still your favorite, aren't they?"

He angled her a glance. The mere suggestion of gooey chocolate tempted him to regress about twenty years. "You're the best, Mom."

As they started in the direction of that magnificent and colossal house that he still couldn't believe his baby sister called home, he drew in a slow breath. Sheila and Courtney had gone back to Courtney's office, and they had said they'd be returning to the café after it closed to help them get ready for the TV show. He knew he wouldn't run into Sheila at the house, which was sort of good, but it offered him no particular reason to go back there either.

He gave his mom's shoulder a squeeze. "I think I'll stay out here for a little while. I might as well soak up some of this springtime sunshine while I can, right?"

"That's right." Mom's expression conveyed a complicated mixture of disappointment and hopefulness. "You spend too much time indoors." She slipped her arm from his shoulder and patted his stomach. "I'll see if Tandy will let me ring that big bell when the cookies are ready."

As Mom continued toward the house, Ben shoved his hands in his pockets and ambled off in the opposite direction. It was strange not having the pressures of work weighing on him, and he felt a little useless. This was supposed to be a vacation. Didn't he even know how to unwind and enjoy himself?

Stepping carefully through the mud and who-knew-what-else surrounding the barn, he found himself in the corral on the far side of it. His eyes lit on a bale of hay with fake steer horns attached to one end that he'd seen Adam use for roping practice. He moved closer, noticing a coiled rope hanging from one of the horns.

He glanced around, seeing only wide-open fields with

mountains beyond and hearing nothing but a soft rustling of the trees and a distant baying of a dog. Firming his jaw, he bent down and reached for the rope. Holding the dusty, splintery coil firmly in both hands, he took another look at the dummy. Sure, he'd taken up racquetball to keep his muscles from turning to mush, but he was a far cry from cowboy material. Did he dare give it a try?

Taking a few steps back, he started circling the looped end of the rope in front of his feet, just as he'd seen Adam do. When he had a good momentum going, he raised it up over his head, but instead of twirling like a real cowboy's lasso, it thwacked him on the back of the skull.

"It's not as easy as it looks, is it?"

Ben snapped his head toward the deep drawl from behind him and saw Hank sauntering out of the barn carrying a bucket.

Great. It was bad enough he had to always feel like a dork. Why did he seem to attract spectators to corroborate it?

"Let me show you how it's done." Hank reached just inside the barn and exchanged the bucket for another coil of rope.

"I appreciate it..." Ben felt like an idiot. He was only going to prove what a klutz he was and make himself feel even worse. What would be the point of that? "...but you really don't have to—"

"It's all right." Hank took a few steps and twirled the loop over his head, then tossed it around the horns as if it were nothing. "It's not so hard once you get the basics down."

He retrieved his rope, then moved next to Ben. "You gotta start with holding it right."

Ten minutes or so later, Hank actually had Ben doing

some halfway decent roping. He'd even nearly caught one of the horns in his loop a time or two.

"Not bad for a city boy." Hank nodded his approval. "If you come out here every day and take a few swings, you'll be roping like a cowboy in no time."

Ben smiled, doubting that but appreciating the reassurance. He took another swing. "I won't expect Adam to be hiring me as a ranch hand anytime soon, but it *is* kind of fun."

"It's like anything else—you get better over time. I'm sure it's the same in your job." Hank did a fancy figure-eight twirl to prove his theory before making another easy catch. "What do you do, anyway?"

"I'm a computer programmer." The words came out sounding a little swallowed. Whatever confidence Hank had developed in Ben's prowess would certainly evaporate once the truth of who he was came to light.

"No kidding?" Hank actually sounded impressed. "Must be nice to have computer know-how. We have one over at the bunkhouse, but I barely know how to turn the thing on."

Ben raised a brow. Didn't everyone use computers these days?

Retrieving his rope, Hank went on. "Be mighty handy to be able to order supplies online and write to my nieces and nephews in Billings, but I've been afraid to even touch it."

A thought took hold of Ben as the sweet aroma of chocolate wafted through the air. "I'd be happy to teach you some basics. In exchange for the roping lesson." He wound up his rope and placed it back over the horn the way he'd found it. "I'm sure we can use the computer in the ranch house kitchen, and besides—" he took another whiff "—my mom is baking cookies. Is now a good time?"

"Sure." Hank tossed his own rope over Ben's. "I'm waiting on Liam and Owen to get back from town with supplies. Might as well make good use of my time."

A few minutes later, Ben sat next to Hank at the computer desk in the large cheery kitchen of the ranch house.

"So you're telling me I can look up anything I want just by typing it into this box?" Hank asked.

Ben nodded. "That's right." Hank seemed to respect him as an expert, and that provided a much-needed boost to his flailing ego. "What do you want to start with?"

Hank rubbed his chin. "Well, there's one thing..." He started to type, haltingly and with just his two index fingers.

Ben smiled at his mom as she set the plate of cookies down on the desk next to the keyboard. Taking one, he watched as the words took form.

"'Thornton Springs Realty,'" he read. "You thinking of buying?"

Hank tilted a nod as he reached for a cookie. "I've had my eye on a little piece of property that just went on the market." He took a bite and spoke through it. "You think I can find out more about it on here?"

Ben swallowed. "Sure. Just type in the address if you know it."

His mom patted his shoulder, telling him she'd be in the parlor if he needed her. Ben had to smile, recalling his childhood days when she was pleased as punch if one of the neighbor boys actually came over to see him. What they usually wanted was help with a homework assignment, but Ben was always happy to oblige.

Watching Hank navigate the site, it struck him that his social life really hadn't changed all that much.

A moment later, a photo of a small house with a red barn behind it and snowcapped mountains in the background came up.

Hank squinted at the screen. "That's the place, all right. This little ranch is just what I've always thought I'd own someday."

"Looks awesome. You going to make an offer?"

"Well…I have a plan." Hank straightened. "But there's a problem."

"Oh?" Ben furrowed his brow. "What's the plan?"

Hank rubbed his neck and glanced at the door where Ben's mom had exited. "Be sure you don't tell any of the women. If one finds out…well, you know how that can go."

Ben nodded, fairly certain he knew what Hank meant.

"See—" Hank lowered his voice "—I'm planning on asking Andra to marry me."

"Really? Congratulations." A pain stabbed through Ben's chest. Of course Hank wasn't going to spend the rest of his life alone like Ben. *He* was the kind of guy women loved, just like Adam and Micah and all the rest. Ben cleared his throat. "So that's the plan. What's the problem?"

"The problem is that if I want this ranch, I have to make my offer real soon before someone else beats me to it. I need Andra to see the place first. I've been saving for a long time and I can't afford to lose any money."

"Oh, I get it. You want to decide together where you'll live."

"Right. Andra's not the type of woman who takes kindly to decisions like that being made for her."

A knowing smile tugged at Ben's lips. What woman was? "So I get why you have to propose to her soon. But why's that a problem?"

Hank lifted his hands in a gesture of resignation. "The woman is always working. I mean, I totally support her being in business and all and I know it's because the café is just getting off the ground." He rubbed his jaw and looked at the photo on the screen. "Now, with this TV show happening, there's not much chance I'm going to get a good opportunity soon. I could really use your advice, city boy."

Ben went a little numb. No one had ever asked for his help with anything like this before. "Well. Couldn't you just go into the café and talk to her on her break...?"

"I thought about that." Hank shook his head. "But I can't just propose to her in the alley behind the café. Standing next to the garbage Dumpster and staring out at Beau's Auto Repair Shop. A guy only has one shot at 'the proposal,' and if he doesn't get it right, he'll never live it down."

Ben nodded. He'd really never thought of it that way, but he supposed it must be true. "Look, I wish I could help, but I'm not exactly an expert at romance."

"Yeah, well." Hank shook his head. "What guy is?"

"I don't know, but I'm worse off than most."

"Why's that?" Hank looked sincerely interested.

Was he actually admitting this? It wasn't exactly something he wanted people to know about. There was just something safe about admitting it to Hank, as though he might understand somehow.

Lowering his chin, he spoke through a tightness in his throat. "I'm just a little...afraid of women."

"Afraid?" Hank twisted his mouth. "You mean like a phobia?"

"No...." A relatively unfamiliar need to be understood started to whittle away at his self-consciousness. "I mean it's not like I'm afraid of *all* women. Just certain ones."

"I see." Leaning back, Hank rubbed his jaw contemplatively.

Ben sighed. At work he faced the giants of the software industry daily. Why was he so afraid to talk to Sheila? "Pathetic, right?"

"Actually, that seems pretty normal to me. Look." Hank put a hand on the back of Ben's chair and turned to face him. "Women are just like us, except...well... *different*."

"Thanks." Ben chuckled. "That helps."

"I can give you a few pointers if you want. Show you the ropes, so to speak."

"That would be great, but—" he gestured toward the little white house on the screen "—you've got your own problem to solve."

"Maybe we can help each other." Hank shrugged his eyebrows. "That's the cowboy way."

Ben caught the glint of humor in Hank's eye. "Sure. You give me some tips on how to talk to women, and I'll help you figure out the right time to propose to Andra."

"It's a deal." Hank nodded. "Now, the first step is to learn to give sincere compliments. The next time you see a woman you want to talk to, just start off by telling her you like her clothes or her hair or something. Women love that."

"Clothes and hair." He pondered. That seemed easy enough. But it wasn't as if women had a task bar that he could just click on for reliable shortcuts. His eyes narrowed. "There has to be more to it than that."

Hank shrugged. "That's the first step. I'll tell you

what—I'll buy you a piece of pie tonight at the diner in town. We'll find you some gals to practice on, and then we'll talk about my options."

Picturing the two of them sidling up to a couple of elderly church ladies, complimenting them on their neatly coiffed hair, Ben laughed to himself. At least that might be a start. "Sounds good."

It also sounded safe. Sheila would probably still be in town, but she'd be at either Courtney's office or the café, a safe distance from the diner.

Ben sat up a little straighter. For the first time all week, he felt a confidence that he hadn't felt since last summer. Maybe there was hope for him after all.

Sheila's heart felt like a lead weight as she slid into a booth at the diner. Not even her afternoon spent exchanging emails with major Hollywood players about Mr. Bloom's upcoming movie premiere had kept her mind off Ben. Why couldn't she just admit defeat and move on?

As she reached out to help Courtney ease into the seat next to her, she suppressed a yawn. While staying up half the previous night working on the Abbott account had taken its toll, it had been worth it. Karl had called that afternoon to tell her that Mr. Abbott had accepted the new design with a few minor tweaks. This had been a red-letter day for her—and her assistant—and she was really proud of him.

"This thing tapes on Friday." Sounding apprehensive, Andra plunked a stack of papers down on the table and scooted in next to Janessa on the other side of the booth. "That's only three days from now."

"It's better to get it over with, don't you think?" Janessa looked considerably less confident than she had earlier in the day—before the reality show had moved from "good idea" to "actual reality." "I can't take much time away from school, so I'd rather just do it."

Andra nodded in agreement and Sheila knew just what she was thinking. She was anxious for Janessa to complete her culinary program so she could take over as chef at the café and Andra could focus on the catering part of the business. That had been their plan all along.

"Well—" Andra started to thumb through the papers "—considering that there's really nothing we can do to prepare besides making sure the place is clean and the pantry is well stocked, I guess you're right."

"There is one more thing we can all do." Courtney rubbed her belly and glanced toward the kitchen, no doubt anxious to eat again. "We can pray for everything to go smoothly."

"And for us to win," Janessa added with a grin, which she quickly dropped. "Oh. I guess that wouldn't be right."

"Maybe not." Andra let out a giggle. "But we can pray to do our best."

"Evenin', ladies." Joe, the owner of the diner, appeared with a tray of ice waters. "Say, is it true about your café bein' on TV?"

"It's true, all right, Joe." Janessa smiled sweetly. "Our little place could become famous."

"I've always said it would pay off for the two o' you to dream big."

"Right now I'm dreaming of a piece of lemon meringue pie." Courtney smiled as Joe set a glass of water in front of her. "We all want some if you have enough left."

"Sure do." He addressed Andra and Janessa. "You

ladies just let me know if there's anything I can do to help you out."

"Thanks, Joe." Andra patted the stack of papers. "But all we really have to do is read through the rules and make sure our place is presentable."

"Well, as owner of your buildin', I'll take care of any spiffin' up you need done." He gave them a fatherly wink. "I'll be right back with that pie."

Andra's eye started to twitch as she tucked a wayward strand of hair under her purple paisley headband and flipped through the pages of rules. "I'm starting to get nervous about who we're going to compete against. It could be any restaurant in the whole country."

"It's not going to be just any restaurant," Janessa assured her. "It has to be one that's struggling. Like ours."

"The Golden Pear isn't 'struggling.'" The expression on Andra's face resembled that of a mother who's just been told her baby is homely. "It's just having a little trouble getting off the ground with our limited resources."

"And that makes it perfect for *Food Fight,*" Janessa enthused. "We have to have a financial need to be on the show."

"A financial need and a viable business model." Sheila leaned forward, trying to read what she could from the rules in spite of them being upside down. "So you should expect lots of customers on Thursday and Friday when the cameras are there."

"Right." Flipping through the quarter-inch-thick stack of papers, Andra started to go a little glassy-eyed. "The judges show up on Friday at twelve-thirty. They can order whatever they want from the menu, so we have to be sure we don't run out of anything."

Sheila's phone beeped inside her purse, and her stomach instantly tightened as she recalled her promise to call Kevin. She slipped her phone into her lap as she checked the screen.

Miss u.

Guilt punched her in the gut. Here it was after dinner and she hadn't even thought about him since lunch.

Courtney squinted at the pages with tired-looking eyes. "Do the rules tell you anything about who the judges are?"

"It says 'culinary celebrities.'" Andra's eyes widened. "They could be anybody from the food world."

Janessa ran a finger along a page as she read. "'The four judges will arrive just like regular customers. They'll order, then after they have a chance to taste their meals, the owner and the chef will be brought out to receive the verdict. The judges will visit the two competing restaurants for that episode in the same week. Then, when the show airs, they will reveal which one received the higher score.'" She looked up. "We won't find out if we win for a couple of months."

A small moan slipped from Andra's throat as she pressed her hand to her forehead.

"Don't worry." Janessa rubbed Andra's shoulder. "The worst that can happen is that we'll have a couple of days of super business, then go back to normal."

Andra shot her the kind of glare that only a best friend can get away with. "No, the worst that can happen is that the judges will hate our food and we won't be able to do anything to stop them from announcing it to the whole world."

Sheila tried to ignore the quarrelsome turn the conversation had taken as she tapped out a quick message on her phone.

Miss u 2.

"Not the 'world' exactly," Janessa said gently. "Technically, just the whole country."

Andra's nostrils flared. "And we think this is a good idea *why?*"

"Ten thousand reasons, Andra." Holding up her hand, Janessa ran her thumb across her index and middle fingertips. "Just keep your eye on the prize."

"Right." Andra lifted her gaze as Joe arrived carrying a tray with five slices of bright lemon filling topped with a generous layer of white meringue.

As Sheila watched Joe set her pie in front of her, her phone beeped again. She glanced down.

Thinking about me?

She sighed. How was she supposed to respond? "Actually, no. I'm thinking about pie"?

A contemplative silence fell over the table while Joe distributed the plates, and Sheila attempted to compose another message to Kevin. Technically, she was thinking about him at the moment, so "Yes," while not terribly imaginative, wasn't really a lie.

As Joe stepped away, the bell over the door jangled and Sheila reflexively looked up. *Oh, no. Not Ben.* Making a sound that was a cross between a snort and a hiccup, she grabbed for her water.

"You okay?" Courtney rubbed Sheila's shoulder with one hand while waving Ben over with the other.

Feeling her face start to burn, Sheila nodded and held

the glass of water to her cheek, hoping it would have a cooling effect on her skin or at least serve as a mask to conceal the blush she felt coloring her face.

Ben stuck his hands in the front pockets of his jeans and ambled toward their table.

"Want to join us?" Courtney patted the impossibly tiny bit of seat next to her. "We're here for pie and planning."

"Actually, I'm not staying. I mean, I'm staying, but—" he looked flustered "—I'm here to meet someone."

Sheila's stomach flipped like a gymnast. He was *meeting* someone?

"Oh, really?" The confused disbelief in Courtney's tone would have bordered on insulting if she hadn't been his sibling and therefore exempt from the ordinary rules of keeping one's thoughts to oneself. "Who?"

Ben drew in a deep breath that seemed suspiciously like a stall tactic and made Sheila's palms start to sweat. Had Stephanie arrived? Was that it?

She fidgeted. Even from where she sat she caught a hint of the same spicy aftershave he'd worn to Courtney's wedding. Tears started to burn behind her eyes as her heart sailed back to the reception, when they'd agreed they wanted to keep seeing each other.

She *had* wanted that. More than anything. Sure, long-distance relationships weren't ideal, but he was the kind of guy who was worth taking a risk for, or at least he had seemed to be. Good thing she had found out the truth about him before she'd fallen any deeper.

And now he had the audacity to stand there right in front of her and announce that he was meeting someone. He had to know that would cut into her heart like a knife. How could he look so innocent and be so flat-out mean?

Drawing in a steadying breath, she fought the temptation to throw her slice of pie right at his handsome face.

"So..." Courtney wiped meringue off her lip. "Are you going to tell us or not?"

The bell above the door turned everyone's head as Hank sauntered in, spotted them, removed his hat and headed their way. Andra perked up as though she'd just ingested a shot of espresso.

Ben jabbed a thumb in Hank's direction. "Him."

Sheila felt her cheeks blanch. *Hank?* Adrenaline surged out with a rush of "false alarm" relief.

Courtney chuckled. "I didn't even know you guys knew each other."

"Evening, ladies." Hank glanced at Ben, then lifted an admiring eyebrow at Andra. "You sure do look pretty this evening."

"Pretty?" She blew a strand of light auburn hair out of her eyes. "I look like I've been standing over a stove all day."

"Just goes to show that doing what makes you happy is good for the soul." Hank gave her a look of pure love and admiration.

"Get out of here with your sweet talk, cowboy. Let us get back to work." Andra tilted him a smile as she picked up the stack of papers and swatted him in the ribs with it.

Grabbing his side in mock injury, Hank looked at Ben and subtly angled a nod toward their table. Ben's eyes widened and he jerked to attention, then looked at Sheila. "Uh...Sheila, your hair is really...short."

She ran her hand through the shoulder-length do. It

had been a good six inches longer for the wedding. Was he saying he didn't like it this way?

After a moment of awkward silence, Hank held his hat in front of his chest with both hands. "Well, we don't want to interfere with the work you ladies have to do. If you'll excuse us..."

Watching Ben follow Hank to a table near the front of the diner, Sheila's eyes narrowed. That shy-guy act was really endearing, and he had it down to a T. It made a girl want to reassure him that he was strong and handsome and smart. All the things he obviously knew how to work to his full advantage.

As Andra recommenced reading the rules out loud, Sheila took a bite of pie and pondered. Stephanie wasn't here with Ben, and Courtney had never mentioned her. Maybe she wasn't his girlfriend anymore, but it didn't matter. Even if he were available now, he had proven he couldn't be trusted and wasn't worth dwelling on.

Now all she had to do was convince her heart of that.

A few minutes later, Ben and Hank had both ordered a piece of apple pie, although Ben's mind wasn't exactly on food.

Your hair is really short. Had he actually said that? He might as well have said "Boy, that cross you have around your neck is sure gold."

"You see what I mean?" He spoke to Hank under his breath. "I really can't talk to women."

"Talking to women is just like roping cattle." Hank took a swig of his water. "All you need is a little practice."

"Maybe." Ben sighed, doubting that practice would do anything but add to his list of humiliations. "There's just something about Sheila that makes me freeze up."

The second he said her name, a tiny seed of panic erupted. He'd never admitted his attraction to Sheila to anybody but God, and even that admission had been only in his head. He held his breath, waiting for Hank to let out a guffaw or give him a pitying look.

Instead, he regarded him from under an arched brow as a corner of his mouth lifted. "Sheila, huh? I had a feeling this was about someone in particular." His expression shifted from enlightened to confused. "Hey, wait a minute. I thought the two of you got along just fine when you were out for the wedding."

"You're right, we did." Memories came like screenshots of his time spent with Sheila that week. Horseback riding. Reading *The Great Gatsby* to each other. Dancing into the night as the wedding reception wound down. It had been great. Especially when they had both agreed they wanted to see each other again.

Thinking about it now, he wondered if he had just dreamed it.

He groaned. "Then, before I left for home, it was like she suddenly turned into a different person. Cold as ice. And I have no clue why." That last part wasn't entirely true. He did have an inkling, but he wasn't ready to be that candid.

"Huh." Hank looked thoughtful. "Did you ask Courtney? Women tell each other everything, you know."

Ben shook his head. "I probably should have. But by the time she got back from her honeymoon, I just didn't want to bug her. I decided it was stupid of me to think Sheila could be interested in a guy like me anyway."

Hank frowned. "Why do you sell yourself short?"

"It's hard to explain." He shook his head. "I don't understand women."

"Well—" Hank glanced over at Andra "—you're not alone there, my friend."

Ben drew in a breath. "But now I really have to find the nerve to talk to her alone. I have something important to tell her."

"What is it?" Hank looked pleased as Joe delivered their pie.

Ben paused, waiting for Joe to step out of earshot. "See—" he picked up his fork "—I live in Fresno and she lives in L.A."

"I'm guessing she knows that." Hank slyly looked up from his pie.

"Right." Ben sliced off a bite with his fork. "But my company has offered me a transfer to L.A., which I'm thinking of taking, but the only reason I'd want to live there would be her."

Hank swallowed. "That's great news." He pointed his fork at Ben. "You owe it to yourself to tell her. I mean, if you don't, you'll always wonder, right?"

Ben looked over at Sheila, and his heart rate seemed to increase. There was something about the way the light hit the red highlights in her hair that made him wish he could run his hand through it. He had clung to the memory of how her hair had smelled when they had danced together, and the scent was still fresh in his mind.

What could he do but entrust this to the webmaster of his soul. He closed his eyes and fervently prayed. *If I can't be with her for life, God, can I please just have one more day of good memories with her? Just one more day.*

Opening his eyes, he looked at her again. *Yeah.* What he wouldn't give for just one more day.

Chapter 4

As Sheila steered Courtney's car from the highway onto the road leading into Thornton Springs, she tried to calculate how much sleep she'd gotten the night before. Between thinking about Ben and then catching herself dreaming about him, it had been practically impossible to relax. It hadn't helped knowing that he was sleeping just down the hall.

She stole a glance at Courtney, who still seemed blessedly oblivious to her plight.

"I really want to finish up in my office by lunchtime so we can get home to work on the baby book." Courtney rubbed her belly, which actually appeared to have grown in the two days since Sheila's arrival. "My mom's so excited. She wants to do it like a family tree with pictures from both sides, so she brought a ton of photos with her."

Sheila smiled in encouragement, wishing that a little

of Courtney's energy would rub off on her. She could use it right about now.

"Mama Greene's taking her to The Memory Trail in Helena this morning to get supplies," Courtney continued. "Knowing my mom, they're going to come home with enough things to put together ten baby books."

As they rounded the bend just before the main business section of town, Sheila slowed, surprised to encounter actual traffic. "I know you get a lot of tourists these days, but this is definitely busier than yesterday."

"Definitely." Courtney watched the people bustling around, snapping pictures of each other and the authentic Old West buildings. "I haven't seen this many people around here since half the state showed up to see Micah compete in our rodeo last summer." Her attention shifting, Courtney pointed to an empty parking space directly in front of the ice cream parlor. "Oh, great. Doris Day parking right in front of Moo."

Driving at a snail's pace to accommodate the flow of cars, Sheila turned her head at the cross street, surprised by the sizable crowd spilling out onto the sidewalk in front of the Golden Pear.

"Whoa." Courtney leaned forward slightly. "The cameras aren't even here yet, but it looks like word's gotten out about the café being on TV. I guess this show's more popular than I thought."

"It's popular, all right," Sheila affirmed, "but I suspect most of the women are here hoping to catch a glimpse of Brian Leary." In L.A. she saw this kind of thing all the time. Women would turn into completely alien creatures at the suggestion that Johnny Depp or Robert Pattinson might be filming in the area. It was no surprise that they'd gather in a small town to witness the arrival of a charismatic reality-show host.

Sheila made a slight swerve out to the left and was about to pull into the parking place when a sleek black Lexus whipped around the corner of the next block. The unexpected movement caught Sheila's attention, distracting her just long enough to give the Lexus time to make a U-turn in the middle of the intersection and zip into the open parking space in one smooth motion, stopping on a dime.

"Hey!" Sheila let out a huff as her inner L.A. native bumped her relaxed vacationing self out of the driver's seat. "I thought I came to Montana to get away from things like that."

Courtney rasped out mock affront. "I thought you came to Montana to see me!"

"Oh…" Reminding herself to lighten up, she smiled at her friend. "That, too."

A shriek went up from the crowd at the café, and Sheila looked to see three or four of the women bobbing up and down in an apparent attempt to get a look at whoever was going to get out of the car.

"People go nuts at the thought of seeing a celebrity." Shaking her head, Sheila continued up the block and pulled into a spot near the corner. "Like they're not just regular people."

"They're not." Courtney coated the words with a thick layer of cynicism. "Plastic surgery, eight-hour days at the gym, hair plugs and tummy tucks. Not to mention the designer wardrobes and food prepared by personal chefs. Nope. Nothing 'regular' about that."

Sheila sputtered out a laugh as she shut off the engine. Courtney would know that as well as anyone, having worked as personal assistant to more than one mega-superstar movie actress.

Undoing her seat belt, Courtney awkwardly twisted

her upper body to watch the scene unfolding up the street. The group of women had worked their way to the corner and now hovered on the edge of the curb, waiting for the driver to exit the Lexus.

Sheila watched as a full head of gorgeous mahogany-colored hair emerged from the car and rose up to a statuesque height. Clearly aware that she had an audience, the woman turned and gave them a little wave, an unmistakable indication that she was accustomed to being observed. The onlookers all visibly deflated, clearly disappointed that their quarry hadn't turned out to be Brian Leary, a recognizable celebrity or even male. They discontentedly retreated back toward the café, presumably to carry on with their vigil.

"Who is she?" Sheila squinted to get a better look as the woman, seemingly unaffected by the crowd's reaction, scanned the town like Anne taking in her first sighting of Green Gables.

"I don't know. . . ." Courtney pressed her nose to the window.

The door to the offices upstairs opened and Mr. Bloom appeared, his smile gleaming. He moved toward the car as the woman whirled to face him, then shut her door and all but ran to throw herself into his open arms.

Courtney made a choking sound, as if her mouth couldn't keep up with her mental response. "I know exactly who that is. *That's* Mr. Bloom's producer friend."

"What?" Sheila studied the beautiful Rita Hayworth look-alike who had wrapped herself around Mr. Bloom as if he was her dearest friend. "But I assumed Blair was a man."

"So did I." Despair filled Courtney's voice, as if she took this turn of events as a personal failure. "I should have realized sooner."

"Of course...." Sheila put her hands on the top of the steering wheel and leaned forward to see past the cars parked between them and the scene playing out in front of Moo. "That's Blair Newman. She's a producer for the Food Lover's Network. I've seen her at restaurant openings. She's a big deal on the food-entertainment scene in L.A."

Blair was almost as tall as Mr. Bloom and slender without being skinny. She was dressed in pants and a short tailored jacket in a shade of pink that Sheila ordinarily detested but that set off Blair's porcelain skin. Her hair fell in thick waves to just past her shoulders and swept back from her face in a way that appeared to be natural but had probably taken great effort to achieve. But the thing that really struck Sheila was that from this distance she looked about thirty but was probably closer to fifty.

Courtney's head bobbed. "I read all about her back when I was researching Mr. Bloom because I wanted to work for him."

"'Researching'?" Sheila tittered. "Is that what you call reading the tabloids?"

Courtney shot her a defensive look. "They weren't *all* tabloids."

Sheila looked at the pair as they talked animatedly and the woman pulled Mr. Bloom into her arms again. "Wow, that hug looks like she means business."

"More than just business, if you ask me." Courtney's words dripped with disapproval. "He dated Blair Newman after his first divorce."

"Really?" She allowed the weight of that information to settle. "How do you suppose your mother-in-law will feel about this?"

Courtney scrunched up her face as though the

thought gave her a pain. "I don't know, but if I were Mama Greene, I'd be keeping a close eye on this situation."

Mr. Bloom gestured toward the café and Blair looped her arm through his as they started across the street.

"Come on." Courtney opened her car door. "They're heading for the café."

Sheila scrambled to grab her purse and to open her own door. "But I thought we were going straight to the office."

"Change of plans." Courtney put a hand on her belly and hoisted her legs out of the car. "We have to keep an eye on things for Mama Greene."

By the time the two of them met on the sidewalk in front of the car and looked up the side street where the café was, Mr. Bloom and Blair Newman had been enfolded into the crowd. Courtney took off like a shot.

"Courtney, wait up." Sheila hurried, wishing she'd opted for her sneakers this morning instead of her beige Prada wedge sandals, which were cute but weren't, at the moment, doing her any favors.

A minute later, Courtney charged purposefully through the door of the Golden Pear with Sheila close behind. Even though Tandy had fed them a breakfast fit for a couple of ranch hands, the rich smell of coffee and baked goods could easily have sidetracked Sheila from their mission. She wavered, with one foot in the line at the counter and a vision of a vanilla latte tempting her sidekick loyalties.

Blair stood with Travis off to one side of the large room. She looked around, smiling brightly and nodding at whatever Mr. Bloom was telling her.

Spotting Courtney and Sheila, he waved them over. Somewhat hesitantly, Sheila abandoned her place in line and followed her friend. Further sustenance would have to wait.

"Blair, I'd like you to meet my assistant, Courtney Greene, and her friend Sheila Macintosh."

Blair reached out an elegantly manicured hand to each of them in turn. "It's lovely to meet both of you."

Sheila shook her hand, somewhat riveted by Blair's beauty. Up close it was easy to see that she was older than she'd appeared from a distance, but there was no trace of the plastic-doll look so common to those who have had "work done." Her nicely tailored suit was made of a good-quality linen. For a moment, Sheila contemplated how Blair managed to look sophisticated and professional in pink, the one color Sheila herself avoided like trans fats. Somehow it always made her feel more ballerina than businesswoman, but she'd abandon that aversion in a heartbeat if she could pull it off the way Blair did.

"Welcome to Thornton Springs." Courtney's voice sounded uncharacteristically clipped.

"Thank you. Travis has been telling me about this place ever since he moved here." Blair turned her red-lipstick-emblazoned smile on Mr. Bloom. "What has it been, Travis, almost two years?"

"Hard to believe," he confirmed.

Courtney pursed her lips with disapproval.

Mr. Bloom appeared unaware of Courtney's apprehension as he gestured toward Sheila. "Sheila is a professional restaurant designer from L.A. In fact, she helped with the design of the Golden Pear."

"How wonderful." Blair looked sincerely impressed. "I'd love to get some of your thoughts on camera about your process."

"Oh…sure," Sheila stammered. The idea of appearing on camera fluttered around in her head, not quite landing anywhere in spite of her outward willingness.

"You can give a plug for your firm." No doubt accustomed to reading between the lines, Blair seemed to sense her hesitation. "Which one do you work for?"

"Maples and Associates."

"Wonderful. I've met Claude Maples. Such a talented man. I'd be more than happy to promote his business on our show." Blair looked around again. "I can see great potential here." She looked at Mr. Bloom and put her hand on his arm in a possibly but not necessarily flirtatious manner. "Oh, Travis. You are a genius. Thank you for talking me into coming here."

Sheila traded a glance with Courtney, sensing that she'd picked up on Blair's intimation that Mr. Bloom had done the convincing, not her.

While Mr. Bloom escorted Blair up to the counter, bypassing the line like a couple of VIPs at Disneyland, Courtney folded her arms as best she could.

"Did you hear that?" she stage-whispered. "She talks like they're best friends."

"Well, Court. Maybe they *are* friends. There's no law against that."

Courtney shot her a sideways glance. "If they're such good friends, why does he never mention her?"

Just as Sheila was about to point out that he *had* mentioned her just yesterday, her phone chimed a poorly timed announcement of a text. Grunting, she reached into her purse.

Courtney eyed her phone. "Everything okay?"

"Oh…yeah." Sheila pulled in a breath at the sight of Kevin's name. She flashed Courtney a quick look that she hoped would communicate her need for a minute of privacy. "I'll just be a second."

Courtney twisted her mouth. "Okay, I can't give you too much grief. I used to be married to my job, too. Trust me, I'd rather be married to Adam."

"Uh-huh." Not bothering to correct the assumption that this was work related, she read Kevin's message about a sale he'd just made. Skimming the text, she shoved aside a vague disinterest.

What was wrong with her? It was great that he was passionate about his work and that he liked to tell her about it. It must just be selfishness on her part to think that he should ask her how her vacation was going before launching into stories about himself.

Still, shouldn't he at least ask a question or two? How Courtney was doing, maybe? Or if her handsome brother had unexpectedly made the trip out from Fresno…?

She stomped down that thought, clearly in need of a strong shot of espresso to set her thinking straight. Of course Kevin wouldn't think to ask something like that, since he had no idea that Courtney even had a brother or that Sheila might have harbored any hidden hope that…

Her finger hovered over the pad. What was she thinking? She didn't harbor any hidden *anything* with regard to Ben. He was a nonissue. Put in the past where he belonged.

Best to keep her focus on Kevin. They were a couple now…or almost, anyway. She needed this time to see where they were headed.

She tapped out what she hoped would come across as an enthusiastic response, then slipped the device back into her purse as she crossed over to the pastry case, where Courtney stood surveying Blair and Mr. Bloom.

Courtney's eyes narrowed to slits, and an unexpected insight caught Sheila in its grip. *Thank you, Lord, for keeping Courtney's attention fixed on Blair Newman and not on me.*

It would definitely not make her life any easier to have her best friend catch on that she was fending off a ridiculous attraction to her brother.

Sitting at a table in the bay created by three practically floor-to-ceiling parlor windows, Sheila traced inside a heart-shaped template onto a photo of Courtney and Adam. She pretended to lose herself in the activity even though her awareness of Ben, upstairs painting the baby's room with his dad, wouldn't quite leave her alone.

As she picked up the photo and started to cut on the line she'd drawn, a loud noise followed by an "Ow!" snapped her focus to the arched doorway leading to the foyer.

Mrs. Jacobs and Mrs. Greene barely flinched, but Courtney looked alarmed. "Mom." She spoke firmly to get her mother's attention. "Maybe one of us should go check on Dad and Ben."

"I'll go in a minute." Mrs. Jacobs put the finishing touches on a paper cutout crib she'd been carefully crafting. "You know how the two of them are when they're working on a project."

"I know. That's why I think one of us should check." Courtney broadened her focus to include Sheila and Mrs. Greene. "My dad gets really *creative* when left to his own devices."

"There's nothing wrong with a little creativity." Mrs. Greene gave her signature warm smile as she traced the shape of a baby rattle onto a piece of butter-yellow craft paper.

"There is when it falls into the wrong hands." Grabbing one of the chocolate chip cookies her mom had made, Courtney gritted her teeth. "When I was little, my dad decided to paint an *Aladdin* mural in my room. It wound up looking like something Picasso would have done on a really bad day."

"You loved it at the time." Mrs. Jacobs peered somewhat defensively over her glasses.

"Only because Dad was so proud of it." Courtney chuckled. "I'd just hate to think of what he could do with my baby-room ducky theme. He might decide to try his hand at an abstract pond."

"Oh, Courtney." Applying a piece of tape to the back of the crib, her mother shook her head.

"This is such a cute picture of Courtney and Ben." Mrs. Greene maneuvered one of the photos on the table to get a better look at it. "How old were they?"

Angling her head, Mrs. Jacobs made a cooing sound. "I love that one. Courtney was in the little strawberry romper I made for her, so she would have been almost two. And Ben is holding the microscope he'd just gotten for his fourth birthday."

"Oh, my gosh." Courtney laughed and reached for the picture. "I totally forgot about that thing. He used to carry it around with him everywhere."

"A microscope?" Sheila tried not to look at it or to dwell on her curiosity over what Ben looked like as a child.

Oblivious to her reluctance, Courtney held up the photo of two sandy-haired kids, one an adorable little girl and the other a boy with black-rimmed glasses and a cowlick. "Other kids carry around teddy bears or blankets. My goofy brother carried around a microscope. What a nerd."

Mrs. Greene tittered. "How long did that phase last?"

"Phase?" Courtney's voice lilted with playful derision. "He's still a nerd as far as we're concerned."

"Now, Courtney. That isn't nice." Her mother regarded her from under an arched brow. "He's just a little introverted."

"Call it whatever you want, Mom. He's still the kid who always had his nose in a science book while you and Dad were watching my soccer games."

Sheila bit her lower lip, catching another glimpse of young Ben and fighting the urge to ask when he'd turned from nerd to hunk.

"Remember his prom night?" Courtney seemed to be on a roll with the brother bashing.

"No. . . ." Lifting a gaze to the ceiling, her mother considered. "I don't."

"That's because he didn't have one." Courtney turned to Sheila. "He stayed holed up in his room that night because he was totally obsessed with some computer program he was writing."

Mrs. Jacobs spoke to Mrs. Greene with a motherly gleam in her eye. "Bob and I are very proud of him."

Courtney leaned toward Sheila, as if rallying for support. "He didn't even have a date at all until after high school."

The comment lit a match in Sheila's stomach. Not until after high school? *Really?*

"Now, Courtney," her mother scolded. "Lots of people don't date in high school. We think of them as late bloomers."

"True." Courtney giggled. "We're still waiting for Ben to bloom." She paused, then shifted gears. "Which reminds me, Mr. *Bloom's* producer friend arrived this morning."

"Nice segue." Sheila raised a half smile, fully realizing how concerned Courtney was about leaving Blair alone with Mr. Bloom. She'd practically had to drag Courtney from her reconnaissance maneuvers when they'd finished up at her office earlier this afternoon.

Courtney flicked her a plea for support as she continued to address Mrs. Greene. "Have you talked to him today?"

"Yes, just after lunch. He was taking Blair over to get settled at the Elkhorn Inn, so we didn't talk long." Her face perked up as if she'd just remembered something. "Oh, girls, before Janessa comes home, we have to show you the beautiful album we bought for her wedding shower." She scooted back her chair and crossed to the settee, which was piled with bags from the scrapbooking store.

Courtney exchanged a look with Sheila, then spoke up again. "You know, Mama Greene, with another wedding coming up, people are bound to start asking you about your plans."

"My plans?" Mrs. Greene wrinkled her brow as she retook her seat, placing a so-white-it-practically-glowed album on the table.

"Oh, you know." Courtney's interest in the book seemed as contrived as the innocence in her tone. "You and Mr. Bloom."

"Travis and I don't have any *plans*." Mrs. Greene let out a small laugh. "We enjoy one another's company. That's all there is to it."

Mrs. Jacobs riffled through the colorful papers in front of her. "You mean you haven't even considered remarrying, Elena?"

"Oh, no." Mrs. Greene batted off the thought like a pesky fruit fly. "We've both been down that road, and neither of us feels the need to make the trip again."

"So..." Courtney returned to the picture she'd been trimming. "Does that mean you could see other people?"

"Sweetheart—" Mrs. Greene closed the wedding book and slipped it back into its bag "—I'm long past that stage of life."

"And Mr. Bloom?" A slight quiver in Courtney's voice betrayed her concern. "Is *he* past that stage?"

Suspicion filled Mrs. Greene's eyes as she sorted through a stack of pictures. "Why the sudden interest?"

"Oh." Courtney shrugged. "No reason." She held another beat. "So you haven't met Blair yet?"

"No, but I invited them both over for dinner."

"Both of them?" Courtney shifted in her chair, looking uncomfortable.

"That's right." Picking through her assortment of craft scissors, Mrs. Greene chuckled. "You know how men are. They always appreciate a home-cooked meal."

"But—" Courtney tossed Sheila a look of mild alarm "—you do know that Blair isn't—"

"Oh, look." Mrs. Greene's attention flitted to the window as a bronze-colored pickup truck appeared in the distance, kicking up a cloud of dust as it approached. "That's them now." She stood and started for the foyer before Courtney could finish informing her of the important fact that would no doubt become obvious within the next few minutes. "I've never met a television producer before. This should be fascinating."

"In more ways than one." Speaking under her breath, Courtney put her hands to her temples.

Mrs. Greene exited the parlor, passing Ben on his way in. Sheila bit her lip and did her best to focus on the photo in her hands, as if the fate of the world rested solely on her cutting exactly along the line she'd drawn.

"Hey, Courtney." Ben looked mind-bogglingly adorable in his paint-splotched jeans and T-shirt, which he'd obviously brought with him from home in anticipation of this project. "You might want to go upstairs and take a look at what Dad's planning to do."

"Oh, no. It's not another mural, is it?" She balled up her fists. "Don't tell me. Ducks swimming in a pond?"

"Not exactly 'swimming.'" One side of his mouth twisted up in amusement. "Try flying. It's more of a Sistine Chapel effect."

"He's painting the *ceiling?*" She gave Mrs. Jacobs a pained look. "Mom!"

"Don't worry, sweetheart." Mrs. Jacobs patiently set down her scissors and pushed back her chair, obviously used to playing mediator. "I'll go talk some sense into Michelangelo."

As Mrs. Jacobs headed for the stairs, Sheila tried to shift her attention off Ben and back to the window. The pickup had pulled up next to the house, and Mrs. Greene stood at the top of the porch steps waiting for her guests.

"What do you think she's going to do?" Sheila asked.

"If she's upset, she won't let on." Courtney shook her head. "We really should have told her."

"What's going on?" Ben moved around behind their chairs to have a look out the window.

Sheila's heart galloped in her chest like a wild horse trying to escape its pen. He had to know how his standing so close affected her. Didn't he? Her face started to heat and she took in a slow breath, hoping somewhat unrealistically that the movement of air would have a cooling effect on her skin. She forced herself to focus on the drama about to unfold on the other side of the glass.

Courtney kept her voice low. "Mama Greene is in for a surprise."

Ben pulled aside the lace curtain as Mr. Bloom walked around to the passenger side of his truck. "What kind of surprise?"

Mr. Bloom opened the passenger door, and Blair swung her mile-long legs out of the truck.

Courtney sighed. "*That* kind of surprise."

Sheila sighed. Not only was Blair Newman gorgeous and elegant in a supermodel kind of way, but she looked exactly like the kind of woman who would date a big-time film director. A pang of concern crossed through her for Mrs. Greene, who stood frozen in position with her back to the window, making it impossible for them to read her expression.

Blair flashed a friendly smile as she and Mr. Bloom started up the walk.

"This is terrible." Courtney moaned. "What if Mr. Bloom is moving on because he thinks Mama Greene isn't interested?"

"But she says she *isn't*." Sheila spoke softly, well aware that Ben could hear every word.

Courtney gave her a look. "That's what she says, but I don't think that's how she really feels."

Ben put a hand on his hip, shifting his weight to one foot. "What are you two talking about?"

Courtney fairly whispered, "The love triangle."

From the corner of her eye, she saw Ben flinch, as if surprised by the answer. He looked outside again, shaking his head. "You're not playing matchmaker again, are you, sis?"

"Again?" Courtney sounded defensive. "Look, I

never set out to matchmake. It just seems to happen that way."

Uncomfortable with the direction this was headed, Sheila watched Mrs. Greene greet her guests. "You know, Courtney—" she calculated her words "—sometimes people are attracted to each other, but romance just isn't a good idea."

Releasing the curtain, Ben took a step back. He had obviously heard her. Had he gotten the message?

"Maybe." Courtney spoke with that sometimes-annoying defiance of the happily married. "But I think Mama Greene just needs a little prodding—"

She was cut off by the sound of the front door opening and voices wafting in from the foyer.

"Elena. I've heard so much about you and your wonderful family." Blair sounded cheerful and sincere. "Travis has been talking about you for months."

Courtney looked at Sheila and whispered, "Months? He's known Mama Greene for two *years*."

"Well, I'm very flattered." Mrs. Greene's voice was calm and steady, not at all like the voice of a woman who felt romantically threatened. "Please come in and meet my daughter-in-law and our guests."

As the three of them entered the parlor, Sheila noticed Courtney eyeing Blair with a narrow, distrustful gaze. She was probably right about her having an interest in Mr. Bloom, but truthfully, she seemed really nice. Sheila wasn't seeing anything underhanded in her approach, and after all, Mrs. Greene hadn't laid a claim on him. It wasn't as if he were off-limits, really.

She watched as Ben crossed to Blair, holding up his paint-covered hands in an explanation of why he couldn't offer to shake. Without intending to, Sheila pictured him wearing nerd glasses and clutching a microscope and she almost laughed out loud.

Then her chest squeezed. Why couldn't he still be that sweet guy who hadn't even had a date until after high school?

Chapter 5

All through dinner, Ben had been so involved in a mental Ping-Pong match over whether or not to talk to Sheila about his job that Tandy's beef stew and chocolate cake might as well have been oatmeal. Now, as he trailed behind the Greenes and their guests on their way from the dining room into the parlor, he said a little prayer. He'd devised a plan, but if he decided to go through with it, he was going to need some divine guidance.

Ever since his conversation with Hank the previous evening, he'd been building up his courage. Then Sheila's comment that afternoon about romance not always being a good idea had crashed his confidence like a computer virus. Should he reboot by telling her about the transfer possibility, risking the pain of a lukewarm rejection? Or should he just forget about it and accept his fate as a permanent bachelor?

He swallowed hard against the lump of self-doubt that lodged in his throat, and hung back with his dad and Mr. Bloom as the ladies chose their seats.

"I'm sure you heard about the movie that was filmed here at the ranch." Addressing Blair, Mrs. Greene smoothed her skirt behind her and sat on one of the little antique-looking sofas. "But it's just as exciting to have a reality show shot in our town."

"We prefer to call it a 'cooking competition.'" Blair sat in a fancy high-back chair opposite the sofa. "The integrity of reality shows can get a little dicey."

"Integrity is important in all areas of life." Mr. Bloom stood behind the chair that was situated between Blair and Mrs. Greene, waiting for Janessa to be seated on Blair's other side. "It's a special responsibility for those of us in the entertainment industry, don't you agree, Blair?"

"Absolutely. We take pride in our show's honesty."

Ben's dad helped Courtney settle onto the sofa next to Mrs. Greene, then joined Mom over near the fireplace. That left only Ben and Sheila standing. Their eyes met and he gave her a smile, which she politely returned before taking a seat next to Courtney.

His heart lifted. She had smiled, albeit in a manner that could have been interpreted about a hundred different ways. It wasn't exactly the meet-me-on-the-front-porch-in-five-minutes kind of smile he would have liked, but it was something, and right now he was clinging to every "something" that came his way.

Feeling restless, he moved over to where the women had been scrapbooking earlier and sat down. They'd left everything all splayed out on the table, just as his mom always did at home when she worked on a project like this. Glancing at the photos in front of him, he mentally reviewed his plan.

Sooner or later, Sheila would say good-night and head upstairs. All he had to do was "coincidentally" go up at the same time. Even if everyone retired en masse, he and Sheila were the only ones staying on the third floor. That would guarantee him at least two minutes of one-on-one conversation—all he'd need to gauge if there was a chance of getting back into her good graces. He smiled to himself. It was a practically foolproof plan.

As long as he didn't lose his nerve or say something completely stupid.

Right.

"It's a shame that Adam didn't make it in for dinner." Mrs. Greene sounded both concerned and apologetic. "This is such a busy time of year for the ranch."

"Yes, I'm looking so forward to meeting him." Blair shifted her focus to Courtney. "You must be happy to have your family here right now, especially with your husband being so busy."

Courtney responded with a curt nod. "Adam will probably spend the night in his truck again, keeping an eye on our mama cow that hasn't had her calf yet."

Ben had noticed that his sister seemed to have abandoned her usual "way" with people around Blair. He shrugged his eyebrows. Must be a hormonal thing.

"So—" Blair crossed her legs "—what happens if you go into labor and the calf hasn't been born yet?"

"One of the ranch hands will take over with the cow." Courtney lifted her feet onto a footstool in front of her. "Adam normally likes to be out there in case there's a problem, but he's got guys he can depend on."

Glancing down at a partially covered picture of Courtney as a kid, Ben huffed out a little laugh. He pushed aside the paper that was covering its other half, and his face fell. It was a picture of the two of them, back in his "awkward phase." The one that had lasted twenty-eight years and showed no signs of coming to a close.

He sighed. It was humiliating that he was such a geek. Toting a microscope around the way other kids carried teddy bears. As if he thought he was going to make some great spontaneous scientific discovery and might need the thing. Other kids had thought he was weird. How old had he been when he had finally realized they were right?

It wouldn't be so bad that his mom brought it to put in the album, but it had been right here in front of where Sheila had been sitting earlier. That meant that she'd seen it and had probably had a good laugh over it with Courtney. *Great.*

He rubbed at a threatening headache in his temple. If there had been any doubt in Sheila's mind that he was a loser, that was certainly gone now. *Thanks, Mom.*

He shifted his focus back to the conversation, which, not unexpectedly, had turned to *Food Fight.*

"When will you start filming, Blair?" Mrs. Greene asked.

"My B-roll team arrives tomorrow, along with Brian Leary."

Janessa perked up. "The women in town are just dying to see him."

Blair gave a little smile. "Women do love him, that's for sure."

"What exactly is a 'B-roll team'?" Leave it to Dad to want to know all the details.

"That's the crew that shoots secondary footage." Blair turned her head to answer Dad but then made sure she included everyone. "My cameraman, Todd, will be my right-hand man for the next two days, shooting footage of the café and customers. Then we'll interview the owners away from the café." She inclined her head toward Janessa. "That's what we call the 'bio segment.'"

Feeling too pent up to really get involved in the conversation, Ben looked down at the table again. A photo of Sheila and Courtney that was probably taken when they'd gone to Big Sur a few years ago grabbed his attention. Glancing from the photo to Sheila sitting across the room, his mouth pulled up a little. How could anyone be so captivating?

"So tomorrow the café will be open just like normal." Blair seemed genuinely happy to explain the rules. "Anyone who comes in to eat might have a chance to talk to Brian Leary about their meal and appear on the show. They do need to sign a release saying we can put them on television, of course."

"We have to go there tomorrow, Bob." Mom was so easily enthused, especially about things that involved food. She looked at Blair. "When does the actual competition take place?"

"Friday is D-day." Blair spread her hands open like a fireworks display. "That's when the A-roll team arrives, along with the judges, to film the main event. The café will close at noon. After that we'll have invited friends and family to be background customers while the judges are there."

Seeing a picture of himself that his mom had taken out in their front yard right after his college graduation, Ben contorted his mouth. Those nerd glasses were fine for work, but he sure was glad he'd finally gotten contacts. At least that was an improvement.

As everyone else continued to discuss the show, Ben

overlaid the picture of himself on Courtney's part of the other photo, making it appear that he was standing next to Sheila.

Getting a little more into it now, he slid a plastic heart-shaped template across the overlapping photos. Something about seeing himself next to Sheila encased in the shape of a heart reassured him. Did that make him a romantic? Or just a weirdo?

After a few more minutes of discussion about the show, Janessa excused herself to go study, and Mrs. Greene moved to accompany Blair and Mr. Bloom to the door.

Courtney rose, then teetered as if she wasn't quite balanced. Grabbing her arm, Sheila stood, too, and a surge of adrenaline propelled Ben to his feet. Was this his chance? Or was she going to stay down here to talk to Courtney, leaving him hanging out awkwardly like some dweeb at the eighth-grade dance?

Wavering, he tried not to let on that he was waiting for the girls to make a move while they talked quietly to each other, probably about the alleged "love triangle" that Courtney was so up in arms about. He kept an eye on Sheila, ready to pounce like a cat if she made a move for the stairs.

"Isn't that cute?" His mom suddenly appeared next to him, giving him a start.

Seeing that she was commenting on the photos spread out on the table, his heart jumped into his throat. *Terrific.* Apparently, she had seen that he'd created the heart scene and was probably about to announce its "cuteness" to the room. This was worse than that time in the sixth grade when she'd told her Bible study group about him writing Jenny Blakely's name inside his binder. Would he never escape?

Thinking fast, he grabbed the microscope-nerd shot, pushing aside the heart with his other hand. "Mom, why did you bring this one?"

"What's wrong with it?" The corners of her mouth drooped. "I think it's adorable."

"There's nothing *wrong* with it. It's just…"

Sheila moved around the coffee table, prompting Ben to drop the photo and take a clumsy step in her direction. "Uh…Mom, Dad…are you going upstairs now…?"

Regarding him with a wary expression, his mom responded, "It's a little early yet. I think we'll stay down here and chat with Elena." She crossed to Dad. "Don't you think so, Bob?"

"Sounds fine. Courtney?"

Courtney had surreptitiously crept over to the window and was peering through the curtains. She jarred back at the sound of her name. "What? Oh." Letting go of the curtain, she turned to them. "I think I'll go up and see if I can get Adam to answer his cell. I always worry about him out there." She turned to Sheila. "You heading up?"

"Sure." Sheila seemed to be fighting a yawn. "It sounds like we have a big day tomorrow."

As the girls started for the doorway, Ben said a hasty good-night to his parents and attempted to catch up.

"Son." Dad's authoritative tone brought Ben skidding to a stop.

"Uh…" He watched the girls making their way slowly into the foyer. "Yeah, Dad?"

"I've been thinking about the painting idea, the one we talked about."

From the contemplative tone in his dad's voice, Ben knew this could take a while. The girls were almost to the stairs. How was he supposed to handle this without being obvious?

"You're right about showing it to Courtney first." Dad had that far-off look in his eye that he got whenever he attempted to access a creative vision. "I think once the women see the sketch, they'll agree with—"

"Good point, Dad." Seeing that this could easily develop into another endless nursery-design committee meeting, he launched a spontaneous plan B. "Why don't I run up and grab the sketch and show it to Courtney before she goes to bed?"

"Fine idea, son...."

Leaving his dad calling out additional instructions, Ben caught up to the girls, who were moving just slightly faster than water flowing uphill. If he hurried, he could grab the sketch and be back by the time they summited floor two.

Advancing a step past them, he spoke over his shoulder. "I...uh...told Dad I'd show you his new plan for the baby's room."

Courtney frowned. "You did get him to repaint the whole ceiling, right?"

"It's plain white, just like you wanted."

Taking the stairs at a near run, he dashed to the baby's room and glanced around the tarp-covered space. Where had his dad put that drawing? If he didn't hurry, Sheila could easily continue on up to the third floor without him.

Seeing the paper peeking out from under a paint can, he grabbed it and dashed back out into the hallway just as the girls hit the top step.

"Here." He stretched out the word in an attempt to cover how out of breath he felt from his jog down the hall.

Looking up at him from under a skeptical brow,

Courtney took the drawing. Instantly, her scowl melted into a smile. "Ohh…it's so cute."

Sheila leaned in, smiling approvingly at the sketch of a yellow duck waddling along with a pair of ducklings trailing behind her.

It pleased him that Courtney liked it, but to see Sheila approve sent a thrill through him. "So I hope you like it, because I—"

He was cut off by the sound of Brahms's Lullaby, and Courtney reached into her pocket to pull out her phone.

Catching on that it was Adam on the line, he and Sheila both turned away as Courtney took a few steps down the hall for some privacy.

His heart went into a humiliating hyperdrive. This was it. The opportunity he'd been waiting for. His mouth opened, but nothing came out, as if the files in his head were too fragmented to efficiently access. Was it possible for the link between a person's brain and their vocal cords to shut off like an internet connection after a power surge?

Sheila backed up a step, her beautiful eyes dancing from side to side like a pair of brown-and-gold-flecked butterflies. The movement gave the impression that she was nervous, too. As though she wanted to let her gaze land anywhere but on him.

He shifted his weight, ready to move with her if she started for the stairs. A slow breath did little to lower his heart rate, but the brain-to-voice connection seemed to reestablish itself just as she spoke, too.

"It really is cute…"

"I don't understand…" He let out a nervous little laugh as she gave him a go-ahead hand. "I don't know why Court didn't like Dad's flying ducks."

"It wasn't the ducks she objected to." She grabbed

her elbows. "It was the duck *hunters* he had hiding in the bushes. That would have given her kid nightmares."

Ben let out a chuckle. "He was thinking it would be like Elmer Fudd and Bugs Bunny. Totally old-school."

"Your dad can be so avant-garde."

"I'll say."

Sheila nodded at the paper still in Courtney's hand. "I didn't know your dad had actual artistic talent."

"Well, he… I mean, I—"

"Hey, Ben." Holding her phone away from her ear, Courtney took a few steps toward them. "I really need you to do me a favor. Tandy is packing up some dinner and a carafe of coffee for Adam, but he doesn't want her to drive all the way out to the north pasture by herself. Would you drive her?"

"What, like *now?*"

"Yeah." She handed him the phone. "He can tell you how to get there."

He looked over at Sheila, who hesitated for a moment before bidding them good-night and making a move for the third-floor staircase. Feeling his perfect plan slipping from his grasp, he took the phone.

Great. Ordinarily, he'd be more than happy to help out his sister, but why did her timing have to be so incredibly rotten?

After tossing around in her big hand-carved oak bed for almost an hour, Sheila gave up and let out a groan. She was due for a good night's sleep, but knowing that Ben hadn't come up the stairs yet had somehow prevented her from nodding off.

It had occurred to her, as they were waiting to say good-night to Courtney and talking about ducks, that she needed to do everything she could to keep from walking up to the third floor with him alone. Sure, it was only one flight of stairs, but she didn't trust herself not to get swept up in conversation and forget why she was so mad at him. He really was just that charming. Thank goodness it had been easy to slip away tonight when Courtney had intervened, but she'd have to be more careful in the days ahead.

Resigning herself to her wakefulness, she sat up and clicked on the lamp, then leaned back into her pillows. While she'd been focused on Courtney, it had been easier to stave off the emotions, but being up here with nothing to do but listen to the clock tick was torturous.

She put her face in her hands, giving in to the rush of memories of the week leading up to Courtney's wedding and the time she'd spent with Ben. Horseback riding. Enlivened conversations. Reading together.

And, of course, the wedding reception. She could practically hear the soft guitar and picture the little lights in the trees twinkling like a million stars. The world had felt as if it were made up of only two people. Sheila and Ben. It had seemed so right.

Lowering her hands, she looked up at the darkened ceiling and sighed.

Please, God. Take away this unwanted attraction and all the pain that goes with it.

She paused, as if expecting an immediate physical manifestation of her prayer being answered. When nothing happened, she folded her arms and slumped lower into the thick pillows.

Now what? After two restless nights, she should be exhausted, but no. She felt as wide-awake as if she'd slept eight hours and had a double shot of espresso. Normally, she liked to read before bed, but knowing how busy she'd be here and how many books there were at the ranch, she'd left her reading device at home. Her mouth twisted as she glanced around the room.

Talk about unfair. There was a full bookcase out in the sitting area, where she and Ben had sat reading together every night of their previous stay, but not so much as a brochure in her bedroom. If she wanted to read, she'd have to risk a close encounter of the Ben kind. Rolling her eyes up to the ceiling again, she spoke right out loud this time. "Lord, are You on my side here or not?"

Accompanied by the tick-tock of what was probably God's silent amusement, she swung her feet to the plush wool rug and padded quietly to the door. Slowly, she pulled it open a crack and peeked down the hall at Ben's open door and the dark room beyond.

Strange that he wasn't back yet. She shook off the worry. It had probably taken some time for him and Tandy to drive to the north pasture, wherever *that* was, and they would surely have stayed at least a few minutes to keep Adam company. For all she knew, he could be downstairs talking to his parents and eating more of those yummy cookies his mom had baked yesterday. Whatever he was doing, it was none of her concern.

Setting her sights on the bookcase on the far side of the sitting area—which was really a wide place in the hallway, with a fireplace and a couple of nice big windows, that separated the two wings of this floor—she ventured a step. All she had to do was make it to the bookcase and grab a book, then hurry back before Ben came up the stairs. It wouldn't take more than forty-five seconds, as long as she wasn't too selective.

Just as she took another step, the creak of a floorboard sounded from the stairwell straight across from her. Alarmed, she scampered back into her room and quickly shut the door, then placed her ear against it. Even over the sound of her drumming heart, she definitely heard someone—Ben?—coming up the stairs. She shut her eyes and strained to listen.

The creaking got louder as he reached the top step, then stopped. Was he noticing the light under her door? Cursing her decision to turn on the lamp, she held her breath, hoping he wouldn't come over and knock. Then the footsteps continued down the hall, and she released her breath.

She leaned against the door, catching a few more indistinct sounds. After a minute or so, she heard a door shut. With a fortifying breath, she pulled her own door open just enough to see that his was now closed and that a thin strip of peachy light emanated from underneath it.

Now was her chance.

Slipping into the hallway, her recollections of the morning after the wedding lapped over her in dizzying waves. She'd left her room then, feeling all swoony from dancing late into the night. On a whim, she'd gone down the hall to see if Ben wanted to walk downstairs to breakfast with her. When she'd held her hand up to knock on the door, she'd heard his voice.

My plane lands at about two-thirty.

Realizing he was on the phone, she'd lowered her hand, debating whether or not to wait. Before she could decide, he'd spoken again.

No, I don't need a ride. My girlfriend, Stephanie, is picking me up.

Her stomach had dropped. His *girlfriend?* The word had hit with the force of a hurricane. Ben Jacobs, the man she had fallen for with every fiber of her being, would never be hers. Not only that, but he had played her in the worst way. He had stolen her heart with no intention of giving her his in return.

He'd laughed then—that wonderful sound that had been like music to her all week had suddenly felt like a knife plunging into her heart. Feeling dazed, she'd wavered, not wanting to hear more but unable to step away.

I know. I've missed her, too. We've been apart for a whole week.

Remembering that now, Sheila's chest throbbed. Talk about feeling duped. She had retreated to her room to finish packing while keeping an inevitable crying jag at bay. She'd missed breakfast—who wanted to eat in the face of a major heartbreak, especially with the cause of that heartbreak sitting right across the table? It had been all she could do to keep from crying as she sat in front of him in Janessa's truck on the way to the airport. Had she even said goodbye to him before rushing off to find her gate?

Now, as she stepped purposefully toward the bookcase, anger pushed aside her heartache. Just because she was single didn't mean she was a willing candidate for a fleeting vacation romance. And now, of course, she had Kevin.

Seething, she stepped around the settee where she and Ben had made of habit of sitting. She wanted to kick the thing, but instead, she stopped, noticing that someone had left a book lying there as if they had intended to come back to it. Her cheeks chilled at the sight of the same first edition of *The Great Gatsby* that she and Ben had taken turns reading to each other.

She took in a breath. Surely it hadn't been sitting here all these months? No, she was certain they'd put it away.

She picked up the book, feeling its weight in her hands and smelling that delicious and faintly musty scent of the aged paper. Was God telling her He had answered her prayer to remove her attraction to Ben with a resounding *no?*

Her breath came out in a long whoosh. If that was the case, it was more than she could stand.

A noise from Ben's room sent her scurrying back into her own. Leaning against the shut door, she stared at the volume she still clutched in her hands as if she'd stolen it. *Just great.* She'd acquired reading material, all right, but it was the one thing that would only serve to dredge up more of the memories she was trying to squash. So did she return the book and risk running into him, bringing up the potential for a conversational stroll down bad-memory lane, or did she stay put and stealthily return it to its place tomorrow?

Ugh. Her head pounded from her sleeplessness the night before. That was it. She wasn't thinking clearly, because she needed a good night's sleep. Surely if she just read a few pages, she'd be out like a rock, and her perspective would be clearer in the morning.

She moved to the bed and slipped under the blankets, pulling them up to her waist and sitting back against her pillows. With trembling fingers, she opened the book, then looked upward at the ceiling. Fine. If God wasn't willing to eliminate her pointless attraction to Ben, maybe He'd consider a compromise. Fingering the pages of the book, she sent up another prayer.

Please, God. If I'm going to make it through this, at least give me strength to resist that man You made to be so maddeningly appealing.

After getting lost in the story of Jay Gatsby's obsessive love for the flighty Daisy Buchanan, Sheila had slept fitfully the previous night. Her dreams had once again been invaded by Ben—something about the two of them tossing shirts in the air, thanks to Mr. Fitzgerald's vivid imagination. At this rate, she was going to need a vacation to recover from her vacation.

Now, as she and Courtney walked around the corner on their way to the Golden Pear, the sight of a large white van with a huge antenna sticking out of the top and the words *Food Fight* emblazoned across the sides and a line of people leading up to the door of the café gave her hope that at least for a while she'd have something non-Ben-related to occupy her mind.

Courtney let out an audible breath, and Sheila slowed her steps. Ever aware of her friend's impending due date, she didn't like the look of worry on her face. "Are you okay?"

"Yeah." Her tentative tone did nothing to support the affirmative response. "It's just that all this reminds me of what happened when *Breaking Story* came to town. Remember that?"

Sheila rolled a comprehending look at the scene in front of them. "How could I forget?"

She should have seen this coming. Courtney had experienced a near disaster two years ago when the popular infotainment show had done a report on Thornton Springs for *North to Montana.* She had inadvertently told the reporter that Angela Bijou, the star, had instructed Courtney to set her up with Adam. He hadn't realized until he saw the show that Courtney had been asking him out on a date not with her but for her boss. Poor Adam had been humiliated in front of the whole town. The whole country, for that matter. It had almost ended the romance between Courtney and Adam before it had even gotten started.

In spite of her friend's apprehension, Sheila had to

smile. One look at the ring that now adorned Courtney's hand, not to mention her tummy protruding under her pink-checked maternity top, offered a happy reminder that it had all worked out fine for everyone. Even Angela had found a Hollywood ending with her handsome costar, Jeffrey Mark Caulfield, that not even the tabloids had sullied.

"Courtney," Sheila said, "I think this show is a little more reputable than *Breaking Story*."

"I'm sure you're right." She still didn't sound entirely convinced. "But if I wasn't so determined to keep an eye on my mother-in-law's romantic interests, I wouldn't have gotten up so early to come here for breakfast."

"Right." Sheila switched her purse to her other shoulder, remembering why she normally preferred to do her away-from-home reading on a lightweight e-reader. First-edition hardbacks weren't exactly built for convenience, but she had wanted to have it today just in case. Judging from the crowd, this could take a while, and if Courtney got much more involved in her reconnaissance, Sheila might just polish off another chapter or two.

They joined the line of curious customers chatting excitedly and straining to see through the windows. A young woman wearing an ID badge on a lanyard around her neck handed them each a couple of papers that had been stapled together.

Sheila read from hers, "'*Food Fight* Rules and Confidentiality Agreement.'"

"Oh, so we have to sign this in order to be on the show." Courtney gave it a quick glance, then looked around at the crowd.

"Guess so." Sheila read more. "'No cell phones, cameras or recording devices, and no talking to the judges.'

Sounds serious." She took out a pen and signed her agreement, then separated it from the rule sheet.

Courtney drifted closer to the window to get a better look, while Sheila tucked her rules into her purse and shoved her hands in the pockets of her distressed-denim jacket. She shivered against the morning chill. What she wouldn't give right now for a nice vanilla latte to warm her hands.

She glanced through the café window, trying to calculate how many people stood between her and the espresso machine. Not only was the place packed to the gills with diners, but the television crew had strategically placed large lights on stands backed by big screens and various other pieces of equipment. People stood around holding clipboards or mics on poles, and at the center of it all was *the* Brian Leary. He spoke to a couple sitting at a table in the middle of the room with smiles on their faces and forks suspended above their breakfasts. Blair stood behind him, alongside a tall man who towered over them with a camera on his shoulder.

Sheila found herself shifting to get a better look at Brian, just like everyone else. With his open collar, pale blue dress shirt and charcoal-gray jacket, he came off as very *GQ* in a distinguished early-fifties sort of way.

"Impressive," she said to no one in particular. "If you're into that celebrity thing."

Courtney stepped back into line. "No sign of Mr. Bloom."

"Well, that ought to make your surveillance job easier."

Courtney tossed her a playfully defensive look. "I'll just be happy to see a certain excessively poised producer leave town, is all. I have to look out for my family."

The woman from the show came back down the line

then, collecting the signed agreements and speaking to the crowd. "Remember, folks, when it's your turn to dine, please don't dawdle at your table any longer than you normally would. Anyone wearing stripes, patterns, offensive or all-white clothing will be asked to either change or come back later today or tomorrow. And no autographs while Brian Leary is working. He's an artist and he has to focus." That last part was said with such seriousness that Courtney and Sheila looked at each other with restrained mirth.

The door to the café opened and Janessa came out carrying a couple of lidded cups. Much to Sheila's delight, she headed straight for them, offering up the drinks as she neared.

"I saw you two out here and I thought you could use a warm-up while you waited."

"You're a lifesaver." Sheila held her hot cup up to her face, inhaling the delightful aroma of coffee and vanilla. "Aren't you supposed to be at school?"

Janessa gave a quick roll of her eyes. "We're shooting our bios today and tomorrow, so I'm taking a couple of days off from class. I'll make up for it next week. Did you get a look at Brian Leary?" She gestured toward the café, where the focus had shifted to a table full of college-aged women who looked up at the host with complete adoration. "I can see why all the women have been waiting for him to get here."

Courtney sipped her tea and looked through the window with an assessing eye. "He's pretty nice-looking in person."

Sheila scowled. "You two are not allowed to ogle. You're both off the market."

"I beg your pardon." Courtney raised a brow. "We're not *ogling.* We're merely observing."

"*You're* entitled to ogle, though," Janessa chided. "What do you think?"

"Of Brian Leary?" Sheila shrugged. "He's okay, but he's not really my type." They progressed forward a few feet in line.

"I know your type." Courtney glanced around. "You'd pick someone like…him." She nodded toward a guy in a yellow pullover sweater leaning on a car in front of the ice cream store and checking his phone messages.

"Him?" Sheila scoffed. "No way. If I was going to ogle, I'd pick…" Giving a quick scan to what she could see of the main street, she tipped a nod toward a guy in jeans and a gray sweatshirt who had his back to them. Something about his broad shoulders and the way he carried himself made him stand out in the crowd. "That guy." She turned to Courtney and Janessa, satisfied with her selection.

"Him?" Courtney sputtered, holding her hand to her face as if tea had just come out her nose. "You think he's ogle-worthy?"

"Well, yeah…" Her voice trailed off as she turned around to see the guy she'd pointed out cross the street come toward them. He was now close enough that she could easily identify him. It was *Ben.*

She whipped back around, flustered.

"Wait till I tell him." Courtney laughed as though she found this seriously amusing.

"Oh, please don't." Sheila did her best to affect a playful tone to cover up the seriousness of her plea. "You know guys. It'll just go to his head."

"Yeah, right." Courtney let her laughter die off as Ben approached.

Sheila pretended to have an intense interest in the

progress of the line, grateful that her friend's eyes didn't linger on her heated and probably mottling face.

"What are you doing here?" Courtney greeted Ben. "You promised me you'd supervise Dad while he paints the ducks."

"He's finishing the walls on his own, and we'll tackle the little mural this afternoon. I thought I'd see how things were going around here."

He turned his million-watt smile on Sheila, and her knees became putty. All she could do was lift a feeble smile and an even feebler wave. That won her a second knee-weakening grin, and she concealed her inability to speak by taking a major gulp of the potent latte she so clearly needed if she wanted to survive this day.

Thankfully, Courtney appeared to remain unaware of Sheila's arm-wrestling match with cupid as she continued her exchange with Ben. "Okay, but if he so much as attempts to paint a feather without you there to help him, you're going to be the one to paint over it, mister."

He gave Courtney a playful salute.

Sheila swallowed a sigh. If that wasn't the cutest thing she'd ever seen, she had no idea what was. Okay, maybe the sight of him at age four wearing those adorable glasses and clinging to his toy microscope. Now, *that* was cute.

"Hey, Court." Janessa pointed toward the café window. "Let's go snag you that table that's about to open up so you can sit." She turned to Ben as she nudged Courtney toward the door. "You keep Sheila company in line, and I'll bring you a latte."

"Oh…okay." His eyes flitted over Sheila in a way that made her want to run but rendered her immobile.

Just great. Even if she didn't want to involve Courtney, why hadn't she said something to Janessa when she'd had a chance? Then she wouldn't be left standing here with her heart laid bare for Ben to skewer once again.

Watching her two friends disappear into the café, she took a contemplative swig of her latte. As she lowered her cup, her purse slipped off her shoulder, catching in the crook of her elbow and jolting her entire body sideways. She squeezed her cup so hard that the lid popped off and a tidal wave of hot sticky latte sloshed out over her hand and onto the sleeve of Ben's Fresno State sweatshirt.

She yelped, jumping back and causing even more coffee to spill. What a klutz. "I'm so sorry." Without thinking, she reached into her purse and dug around for the packet of tissues she always kept handy.

From the corner of her eye, she could see Ben look down, and her heart took off in double time. The slightly tattered blue cover of *The Great Gatsby* was poking out for all the world, in general, and Ben Jacobs in particular, to see.

He pointed to the book. "Oh, hey—"

"Ben!"

In a display of fortuitous timing, Hank charged up to them with a look of urgency that seemed highly uncharacteristic. He nodded a greeting to Sheila as he continued speaking to Ben. "You got a minute?"

"Oh...uh..." Ben glanced at Sheila, as if hoping she had more to offer him than the flimsy little tissue she held in her hand, but took it anyway. "I guess so...."

He dabbed at his sleeve, probably more to please her than because he thought it would help. Hank gave her a polite but obvious "do you mind?" look, which she took as her cue to go join Courtney.

She turned to go, in spite of that crazy pull of wanting to stay. Why was her heart so confused?

As she scooted through the door and moved through the warren of people and tables, she gave herself a mental reprimand. What a dweeb she was. Spilling her coffee on him and barely even managing an apology. Obviously, Ben had seen that she was toting *The Great Gatsby* around in her bag. What was he going to make of that and why, if he didn't matter to her, did she even care?

Chapter 6

Ben wanted to sing. It seemed like such a small thing, but when he'd gone back out to the sitting area last night and had seen that the book had disappeared, he'd been hopeful. Now he knew that not only had she taken it, but she was obviously reading it. Was she thinking about the times they'd shared, reading and discussing it? Maybe not, but at least it gave him a tiny ray of hope.

Recharged, he turned his full attention to Hank, who was saying something about an urgent call from his real estate agent.

"Another guy wants to take a look at that ranch. If I want it, I have to make an offer *today.* What am I going to do?"

Ben leaned in so he wouldn't have to raise his voice to be heard over the noise of the crowd. "I guess you'll have to ask Andra to go out there with you today. Maybe on her lunch break."

"She owns a café." His voice took on an air of defeat. "She doesn't really take a lunch break."

"Oh, right."

"Plus they're expecting a lot of business today and tomorrow, so they have extra baking to do." Hank removed his cowboy hat and ran a hand through his hair. "She already told me they have to shoot her bio part of the show after the café closes and that's setting her back. She'll be working till real late tonight."

"Look, all you have to do is get her alone for a few minutes...." Ben let the thought trail off. Who was he to give advice about something he couldn't manage to do himself?

"I can't rush it." The lines in Hank's forehead deepened. "If I'm going to propose to Andra, it has to be just—"

A sharp intake of air drew their attention to Janessa, who stood next to them holding Ben's latte and staring up at Hank.

"Did you just say you're going to propose to Andra?" Speaking with barely concealed elation, she shoved the cup at Ben.

"Janessa, keep it down." Hank raised a hand and scanned the crowd for anyone who might be paying attention. "I don't want the world to know just yet."

"So I did hear right." She looked as though she wanted to let out a squeal. "How long do I have to keep it a secret?"

Hank gave her the quick version of his dilemma with the ranch. "So I really need to act fast."

"That place sounds perfect." Janessa clasped her hands together under her chin. "But you're right about Andra wanting to be in on the decision." Her gaze grew momentarily distant, then she snapped her fingers. "I have the best idea." She turned on her heel, calling over her shoulder as she moved toward the door, "Wait here."

Hank shared an uncertain glance with Ben. They watched through the window as Janessa wove around the tables and had a quick animated conversation with Blair, who smiled broadly and nodded at whatever Janessa had said to her.

While that conversation played out, Ben's gaze drifted over to Sheila, who seemed to be engaged in a heartfelt dialogue with Courtney. As she talked, her fingers absentmindedly toyed with the cross she sometimes wore around her neck. Knowing that she shared his faith made the idea of not being able to be with her all the more painful. She was perfect in every way.

Except for the part about not loving him back.

The earlier elation he'd felt about the book cowered under the weight of that thought as the line moved them to just outside the door. A woman handed them each a set of rules and something to sign as Janessa made a beeline back to them.

"Okay, I got it all worked out."

"All what worked out?" After glancing at the form, Hank scribbled his name and handed it back.

Janessa held up both hands as if she were under arrest. "Trust me on this." She leaned in, causing both men to do the same. "I arranged with Blair Newman for you to take Andra to the ranch this afternoon to shoot her bio segment."

Hank tipped his head in consideration, then nodded in approval.

Janessa forged ahead. "It will be perfect. You can show her around the cute little ranch, and they'll capture it all on camera. Andra will love it, because she's dying for something interesting to happen in her bio. This will make it look like her personal life isn't a snore-fest."

Hank frowned. "Hey, her life's not *that* dull."

Janessa twisted her mouth. "She works here six days a week and usually caters on the seventh. Not exactly epic."

Hank rolled his eyes upward. "All right, so I get to show her the ranch today. But that only solves half my problem. I still need some time alone with her."

"You haven't heard the best part." She grinned. "While you're at the ranch and the camera is on you… you find just the right moment to ask her to marry you."

Snapping up straight, Hank turned a little white. "I do *what?*"

"It's perfect." Janessa went on, apparently taking his question to be rhetorical. "Blair thinks it's a radical idea. It will make everyone pull for the Golden Pear to win, and do you know why? Because America loves romance."

Hank looked skeptical. "I don't know if that's quite what I had in mind." He looked to Ben for support. "What do you think?"

Honestly, Ben didn't know what to think. It sounded risky, but if another woman, who also happened to be Andra's best friend, thought it was a good idea, how bad could it be? He gave a confident nod. "I think you should go for it."

"All right." Hank seemed to take his advice to heart, causing Ben to instantly wish he'd pleaded the fifth. "Tell Ms. Newman I'll do it."

Janessa gave him a quick hug and bounded off to seal the deal.

When Ben looked at Hank again, he saw a glimmer

of something resembling fear in his eyes. He spoke softly. “You sure you’re okay with this?”

Working his jaw, Hank looked as if his mind was racing. “It’s just that…” He let his voice trail off as his gaze lit on something inside the café.

Ben looked, seeing Andra, her hair pulled back in her signature head scarf, putting some pastries into the case next to the counter.

“I never really thought about it,” Hank went on in a soft voice, “but what if she says no?”

Ben returned his eyes to Hank. For the first time since he’d known him, he could see the vulnerability under that strong cowboy demeanor. Maybe Hank had been right. Maybe Ben’s insecurities about women were more universal than he’d realized.

“You have nothing to worry about.” He placed a reassuring hand on Hank’s arm. “You know she’ll say yes.”

Hank blinked and looked at Ben, then nodded slowly while the words took root. A cautious smile lifted one corner of his mouth. “All I can say is, you’re going with me today so I don’t lose my nerve.” He stuck out his hand.

As they shook, Ben glanced again at Sheila, who was watching him but quickly looked away.

His heart took a strange little leap in his chest. Something seemed to be telling him not to give up hope. Not yet, anyway.

In spite of her desire to keep a safe distance between her heart and Ben, Sheila had dutifully driven Courtney out to the ranch that Hank wanted to show to Andra, knowing full well Ben would be there, too.

Leaning against the car, Sheila kept a close eye on Courtney as they watched the cameraman trailing Hank and Sheila around the outside of the paint-chipped but still adorable old ranch house. Ben followed a few steps behind, looking as if he wanted to jump out of his own skin.

Shoving her hands in her jacket pockets to stave off the cold spring breeze that kept kicking up, Sheila flicked a concerned glance at her friend. "Don't you think you should be home resting?" It had been a while since lunch, and she knew Courtney had the appetite of an elephant these days. "You could go into labor at any second, you know."

"I'm fine." Courtney directed a cat-eyed glower on Blair and Mr. Bloom, who hung back from the filming, holding up their hands as if they were discussing camera angles. "If I left this job up to you and Ben, you two would wind up under that tree over there reading, and next thing you know, my boss would be front-page tabloid news with the wrong woman."

A rising tide of guilt weighed in against Sheila's already frazzled emotions. She should just tell Courtney what was going on—or what wasn't going on—between her and Ben and get it over with. After all, it would be comforting to be able to rally some support from her best friend.

Gathering up her nerve, she pulled in a strengthening breath.

"Oh, great." Courtney spoke before Sheila had a chance to. She tipped her head in the direction of the barn, where everyone seemed to be headed. "We're on the move." A guttural sound erupted from her throat as she pushed herself away from the car and started to follow the group. "I think they want to film in the field back there. It looks pretty overgrown but, boy, what a view."

Sheila released the air through her teeth, letting the moment go. If she was going to confide in Courtney, best to do it in a moment when she wasn't quite so distracted.

Walking toward the red barn that could have come straight from a Grandma Moses painting, Sheila hoisted her purse onto her shoulder and took in the peaceful scenery. Surely there was a fence out there somewhere marking the border of this sweet little ranch, but from here the expanse of lush golden-green fields seemed to stretch all the way to the distant emerald mountains.

"Boy—" she grabbed Courtney's arm to help her navigate the less-than-flat pathway that wended around behind the barn "—am I ever glad I wore flats today."

Courtney's attention flipped as she watched the group stop near a small grove of trees. "Hey, do you hear that?"

Sheila paused as a faint swooshing sound became more prominent. "Is that the creek? The same one that runs through the Bar-G?"

"It sure is. It's high right now, thanks to the spring thaw." Courtney looked around as if to gain her bearings. "I think we're just up from Aspen Creek Falls. We should go there sometime."

They walked a few more feet, and the snaking waterway came into full view.

Expecting the same serenity of the part of the creek that moved through the Bar-G, Sheila jarred a bit at the movement of it. Here sparkling sequins of rushing white water flowed like shoppers charging purposefully into a sale at Macy's. Frothing and crashing against jutting rocks and downed trees, the water seemed alive with purpose as it hurried by.

But not even that amazing evidence of God's hand

could keep Sheila's eyes from gravitating back to Ben. She watched him bend down and pick something up that turned out to be a rope. While Blair set up the next shot, Ben appeared to be tying the rope into a lasso. He reminded Sheila of a little kid, turning anything into a toy to keep himself from getting bored while the grown-ups worked. That image made her smile.

He glanced over at her with a molten look in his eye that made her think she might just melt into a big puddle of disillusionment.

"So what do you think?" Courtney's voice pulled Sheila out of her thoughts.

"About...?"

Courtney puffed out a long-suffering breath. "I was asking why you think they're filming here."

"It's pretty obvious." Looking over at Andra and Hank as they talked and pointed things out to each other, a rush of warmth filled her chest. She could just see the two of them living out their days here. "They're perfect together, don't you think, Miss Matchmaker?"

"Hey, that's Mrs. Matchmaker, if you don't mind." Looking at Sheila, Courtney's face turned serious. "Is something wrong? You've seemed kind of preoccupied today."

Sheila bit her lip, wanting to tell her but feeling awkward now that she'd put it off for so long. "You know, it's just..." She looked over at Andra, who stumbled on her way down to the creek. Without missing a beat, Hank scooped her up in his arms, and the cameraman was right there to capture the moment. A swoon swept through Sheila's heart. She wanted someone to do things like that for her.

Glancing at Ben, she sighed. "I'm a little confused about a guy, that's all."

Courtney's eyebrows shot up as though they might just fly away. "A guy?" She twisted her head, probably to make sure Blair and Mr. Bloom were in no danger of spontaneously running off to elope or something, then pulled Sheila around to face her. "What guy? Who?"

Sheila stole another look at Ben, who had managed to tie the rope into a loop and was twirling it at knee level. He looked like the hero in an old Western, standing there with the tall grass blowing around his ankles and the fluffy clouds peeking over the majestic mountains behind him. Her breath caught in her throat.

Face it, Sheila. Without the Stephanie factor, there was no way she could make a convincing case against falling head over heels in love with him. Admitting her feelings to Courtney would be like putting out a contract on her heart.

Backpedaling, she blurted out, "His name's Kevin."

"Kevin?" Courtney's face froze in a complex jumble of elation and utter disappointment. "I don't think you've mentioned him."

Sheila's heart sank at Courtney's less-than-enthusiastic response. She had somehow expected her to be a little more supportive. Now she regretted her decision to bring it up.

"It's no big deal." She shrugged, trying to sound blasé. "I met him at a business function. You know, one of those corporate parties where you latch on to whoever can make decent conversation. Kevin sells advertising, and he likes to tell funny stories about the people he meets."

"Oh. . . ." From the sound of Courtney's voice, she clearly was neither amused nor sold. "And you've been *dating* him?"

Sheila shrugged again. "Only for a few weeks."

Why was she downplaying this? It had to be because of her track record with men. More than once, she'd gotten her hopes up, only to be disappointed when the guy turned from Mr. Right into Mr. Super Critical or Mr. No Commitment.

Another look at Ben made her stomach burn. *Or Mr. Totally Unavailable.*

"Sheila." Courtney reclaimed her attention. "Why didn't you tell me? This is big news. And I'm your best friend."

"I was waiting for the right time to bring it up. Besides, we just started dating a few weeks ago. I'm still in the wait-and-see phase."

"Oh." A calm acceptance settled over Courtney's face. "Well, if Kevin is the guy for you, I guess you'll know."

"Cut!" Blair's muffled voice sliced across the distance. "Hank, it's too loud here. The mic can't pick up what you're saying. Let's move back up by the house."

Blair stumbled and reached out to Mr. Bloom, who took her by the arm and led her back up the bank.

Courtney let out an actual growl that made Sheila think she might pounce like a tigress if Blair got too close. She took a step back toward the way they'd come.

Feeling a little unsettled, Sheila hesitated. "I think I'd like to stay out here for a minute. Do you mind?"

Courtney gave her a questioning smile, then nodded.

Watching as Courtney caught up to Ben, who had tossed his makeshift lariat back in the tall grass, Sheila sighed. Somehow that conversation with Courtney hadn't gone the way she'd hoped. *Oh, well.* At least now Courtney knew about Kevin, so even if she did start to entertain any ideas about her and Ben, Sheila would have a line of defense. *I already have a fella, remember?*

She turned to face the creek. Hoping to cleanse her mind of all her cares, she meandered a little farther from the buildings, swerving toward the sloshing water.

Peering downstream, she wondered how far it was to that waterfall Courtney had mentioned. Hard to tell, since the creek disappeared into a stand of trees up ahead, but judging from the speed of the rapids, it was probably pretty close.

A large boulder jutted out over the edge of the bank a little ways up, inviting her to sit and enjoy the peace for a minute or two before heading back. That sure would be a perfect place to wait for a word from God.

She shut her eyes. *Lord, why can't I just be content?*

As she carefully picked her way over the rough terrain, something—probably a pebble—hitched a ride in her shoe and poked the bottom of her foot. Knowing that it wasn't going to work its way back out without a little assistance, she hobbled the rest of the way up to the boulder and sat. *It figures.* All she had wanted was an answer to her prayer, and what she got was a pain in her sole.

Since the weight of the book in her purse was starting to cause a kink in her neck, she slipped the strap off her shoulder and let the bag rest next to her, then pulled off her shoe.

Just as she gave it a good shake, a big wasp launched an air raid right at her face, so close she felt it touch her nose. She shrieked, batting at the unwelcome dive bomber with both hands and sending her shoe flying. It landed with a *splat* in the bubbly water about five feet down, getting caught up in a tangle of fallen tree branches.

"No!" How could she have let this happen?

Keeping an eye on the black shoe bobbing in the current, she climbed off the boulder and onto the rocky precipice that was still a good three feet above the water. At least no one—and "no one" really just meant Ben—had witnessed this act of ineptitude. Still, it sure would be nice to have some help right about now.

Looking around, she assessed her options. All she could see of the ranch now was the barn, which blocked her view of the house and consequently all hope of anyone happening to see her. She had wandered so far that hobbling back for help would be impractical at best. She'd arrive with a very sore foot and a very frazzled ego. No, it was best to handle this one on her own.

She turned back to the creek. This would make a funny story later, but right now all she could think about was retrieving her fifty dollars' worth of designer shoe.

Inching her way to the edge of the drop-off and looking down, she confirmed that there was no place closer to the water to get a foothold. The shoe was only a few inches from shore, but it was too far down to reach without some kind of extension.

She looked around, saw a nice long stick and grabbed it. As she got down on her knees, a fine mist chilled her face. It reminded her of Courtney's comment about the high water being the result of the spring thaw. She shivered. Considering the nip in the air, the temperature of the water had to be substantially less than what she was used to at her condo's heated pool. Keeping that in mind, she got a firm grip on a rock that looked securely embedded in the edge of the drop-off. Leaning over, she aimed the stick at her floating footwear. *God, please help me.*

The tip of the stick easily hooked the inside of the

heel. Assured that this was going to be easier than she'd thought, she stretched her arm just a tiny bit farther.

Just as she was about to lift it up, the dirt around the rock she had a hold of started to crumble away. Flailing, she let go of the stick and tried to grab at the ground, but it was no use. Unable to gain a grip, she felt herself slipping down the bank, then plunging into the freezing current and being carried away. Downstream. *Toward the waterfall.*

Disoriented, she envisioned a small drop. Insignificant. Like a child's slide. Then reality hit like the icy current crashing against her body. Courtney had called the falls by name. The fact that it *had* a name meant that it was the kind of thing you don't go over intentionally, at least not without a barrel and people who love you trying to talk you out of it.

She opened her mouth to cry out for help, but a surge slammed against her face and she was pulled under. Her eyes burned and her mouth filled with freezing water, killing the sound before she could make it.

As the late afternoon ticked its way to early evening, Ben paced next to Courtney's car. Although his eyes were on Hank and Andra taking direction from Blair on the front porch of the house, all he could think about was Sheila. He couldn't say exactly why, but it really troubled him that she had stayed down by the creek on her own.

After catching her looking his way earlier in the café, his feeling of hopefulness had faded in and out like images in a PowerPoint, leaving him feeling shaky and unsure of himself. His initial hope that the excitement of witnessing the proposal would lead to more soulful glances from Sheila had petered out when the stop-and-start reality had set in. Sheila had seemed preoccupied—distant, even—ever since they'd arrived.

Now no amount of glances over his shoulder at the corner of the barn brought her walking around it. He'd thought more than once he should go over there just to make sure she was okay, but that seemed so calculated. It would be just what he *didn't* need for his matchmaking sister to catch on to his feelings for her best friend.

He looked at Courtney, who sat in the backseat with the window rolled down, scowling as she kept an eagle eye on Blair. It struck him as funny that she assumed the woman was after Mr. Bloom just because they were friends. He didn't know if he was insulted or relieved that his sister hadn't made the same assumption about him and Sheila when they'd been inseparable last summer. Evidence, he supposed, that the idea of Sheila and him as a couple was completely unrealistic.

Looking really uncomfortable, Courtney started to fan herself in spite of the cool weather.

He grimaced. "You okay, sis? You look like you could use a glass of lemonade."

"I'm fine." She spoke through gritted teeth, glaring at the sight of Blair consulting with Mr. Bloom over by the house. "This can't take much longer."

He looked toward the barn again. "Let's hope not."

As his gaze swept back across the yard, Hank caught his attention, lifting up his hands in a gesture of surrender. When they'd talked after coming back from the creek a few minutes ago, Hank had expressed frustration at this being more about getting the right camera angle than about his proposal or even getting an accurate depiction of Andra's personal life.

"That's showbiz," Ben had quipped, knowing it wasn't really funny.

It was great that Hank had gotten to show the ranch to Andra, but Ben was having serious second thoughts about the whole public-proposal idea. Now that they were here, it didn't seem very romantic, but then again, what did he know? At this point, he really just wanted to assure himself that Sheila was okay and get Courtney home to rest.

He stole another look at the corner of the barn, but there was still no sign of Sheila. He scratched his head. "Hey, Court. What do suppose is keeping Sheila?"

"Oh, you know her." Courtney's voice sounded as if it were being dragged through Jell-O. "She's probably sitting there thinking and she's lost track of time. You want to go check on her?"

Did he ever. That changed everything. If he was doing it for Courtney, it wouldn't seem suspicious. He straightened like a soldier called to attention. "I'll just let her know we're finishing up here."

"Let's hope that's true." She leaned both arms on the window opening. "I'm ready to go get some dinner."

"Will wonders never cease?" he joked, trying to cover his growing feeling of genuine concern about Sheila.

She swatted his arm and he pretended to let that propel him into motion.

Walking quickly, he took another glance over at Hank. He felt bad about abandoning him, but this shouldn't take long. Besides, of all people, Hank would understand he was being granted another opportunity to talk to Sheila alone.

On approach to the barn, his forehead broke out into a cold sweat. Why did the mere thought of being alone with her send him into a near panic? Trying to calm himself, he shot up a quick prayer. *Please, God, don't let me blow it this time.*

He rounded the corner and stopped, expecting to see her somewhere close by. His eyes darted around, but she was nowhere to be seen. Strange. Maybe she was sitting on the bank of the creek and he just couldn't see her over the tall grass. He started walking again, craning his neck as he got closer to the creek.

Reaching the edge of the water, a quiet tension hit him in the gut. Where on earth was she? Slowly, he continued along the bank of the creek, scanning the landscape. Just as he was about to take out his phone and call Courtney, something caught his eye on the top of a big boulder up ahead. His heart racing, he picked up his pace, panic setting in as his suspicion was confirmed. Before he'd even reached the big rock, he could tell that the object on it was Sheila's purse.

He looked downstream and saw something move midway through the creek several yards ahead, where the water cut around either side of a downed tree. He squinted. It moved again, and this time he saw that it was an arm madly waving.

"Sheila!"

Still screaming out her name, he clambered around the boulder and down to the rocky rim of the creek. He could see her face now, barely bobbing above the water. She had a tenuous grip on the tree. "I'm coming. Hang on!"

Her head turned and she cried out. "Ben! Help me! I…can't hold on…!" Her voice sounded muffled as she jerked in and out of the water.

The urge to jump in after her tugged at him, but he knew he wouldn't fare a whole lot better than she was against that strong current. Then an idea struck.

"Hold on!" Making an abrupt about-face, he started up the bank, calling over his shoulder, "I'll be right back."

Running in the direction from which he'd come, he tried to remember exactly where it was that he'd been standing a while ago. He darted through the tall grass and looked around, frantically searching the area.

Please, God.

There, barely visible in that overgrown thicket where he'd waited earlier, was that beat-up old rope. He wanted to shout. Hurrying, he bent to retrieve it, then ran back as fast as he possibly could, grateful that Hank had taught him how to tie a lasso and that, for some crazy reason, that was what he had done earlier to expel his nervous energy.

Skittering back down the bank, he got sight of her again. "Sheila! Can you hold up your arm? Nice and high."

She faltered, but her arm jutted up out of the water and she held it there.

"That's good," he shouted. "Now keep it there. I'm going to throw this rope out to you, and I want you to grab it." Even as he heard himself say it, the likelihood of his plan working seemed remote. He couldn't do this on his own.

Please, God. Help me out.

He swung the loop over his head, keeping his focus on Sheila. She was no more than ten feet away from him, about the distance he'd stood from the steer dummy. He could do it. All he had to do was get it close enough for her to grab. Remembering everything Hank had taught him, he said another prayer and let it fly.

The loop sailed through the air, landing in the water. For a second, he thought he had missed her—just his luck that it would get tangled in a tree branch—but then her hand shot up and he could see that she had a hold of the loop. *Thank You, God.* His body practically gave out from the adrenaline release.

He called out to her. "Okay, now just pull it over your shoulders and hold on. When you feel like you can let go of the branch, I can pull you in."

As she let go and started to move toward the bank, he held tight to the rope. Worried that the force might jerk him in, too, he braced one of his feet against a big rock and kept pulling. Finally, he could see that she had her footing and could walk the final few feet out of the water.

At the edge, he grabbed her, pulling her to safety. They both fell onto the rocky ground, wrapping their arms around each other. He could feel her soaking-wet body trembling and hear her whimpering in his ear. All he could do was to hold her tight and continue to whisper "It's okay" over and over, confident now that it would be.

Time seemed to stand still as he held her, wanting to never let go, but he had to get her someplace warm. She was out of the water but not yet out of the woods.

As he released her, she sat back, still gasping for air and crying. A breeze kicked up, sending a fresh shiver through her. He tugged his sweatshirt off, thankful for the T-shirt underneath, and helped her pull it over her head.

"Thanks." Her jittery voice seemed thin. "I don't know what would have happened to me if…" She looked out at the rushing creek, then down at the rope still encircling her middle. "If you hadn't suddenly transformed into Will Rogers."

He laughed, rubbing her upper arms. "Hank's been

teaching me how to rope. He told me if I could snag a woman, I'd be ready to move on to cattle."

She pulled the rope off and handed it to him. "Well, watch out, cattle." Her face changed, as if she'd just remembered something. She turned to look upstream. "I left my purse..."

"I saw it." He helped her stand. "That's how I knew you were..." He frowned. "*What* were you doing, again?"

Grabbing her elbows, she glanced down and he followed her gaze to her one shoeless foot. "I dropped my shoe in the water, and I..." Turning a look to the creek and then back to him, concern draped her pretty face. "Do you think you could get it?"

He raised an eyebrow. All this over a lost shoe? He couldn't help the smile that curved his mouth. "I can try, Cinderella."

After securing a promise that she wouldn't move and knowing that she probably would anyway, he maneuvered back down the bank, seeing her shoe stuck exactly as she'd described. It took a bit of effort, but compared to rescuing her from the drink, the shoe was the easy part. A minute later, he draped the purse over her like a Miss America banner and presented the shoe as if it were a trophy.

"Thanks." She braced herself against his shoulder while she forced the shoe on over her sopping-wet sock. "You're currently my favorite superhero."

In his head, he did one of those ridiculous touchdown dances. If lightning struck him right this second, he would die a happy man.

He winced as she took her first squishy step. "It's an improvement, but let's get you to the car so we can crank up the heat and thaw you out. Then I don't care whether Hank's proposed yet or not, we're heading for home."

She stopped and slammed a hand against his arm. "What did you say?"

He let out a groan. This was supposed to be a secret. Of course, it didn't much matter now that it was almost—or maybe even *was*—a done deal.

When he didn't answer right away, she asked a more pointed question. "You don't mean he's thinking about proposing to her *now?*"

A prickle of dread ran up his neck. "Why, you don't think that's a good idea?"

"I think proposing is a great idea, but not in front of a TV camera."

He started to walk, slowly but with a renewed sense of purpose. "But she said she wanted something interesting to happen for her bio."

"Something interesting, not *monumental*." Her steps were careful, but she picked up their pace. "No woman wants one of the biggest moments of her life to happen on a reality show."

"No?"

"No! Unless she's a contestant on *The Bachelor*."

Fire churning in his throat now, Ben looked over at the area where the buildings were and wondered if they were too late to stop Hank from digging himself into a major hole. He looked at Sheila, then grabbed her hand. "Come on."

Together they ran, her shoes making a *squish, squeak* sound with every step she took.

When they came around the corner of the barn, Hank and Andra were standing in the little flower garden in the front yard. The cameraman stood close, as if he was making sure the microphone picked up their every word. Blair and Mr. Bloom stood nearby, watching.

Ben's heart raced. Since Andra wore neither the look of a woman who was newly engaged nor that of one who was recently outraged, he figured they weren't too late.

Not knowing what else to do, he shouted, "Hey!"

When everyone—including, to Ben's dismay, the cameraman—whirled around to face them, he and Sheila skidded to a halt. The looks of astonishment on everyone's faces puzzled him for the half a second it took to recall that his running mate currently resembled a Barbie-doll version of the Creature from the Black Lagoon. Everyone massed toward them, and Courtney popped out of the car like a pregnant cannonball.

The next few minutes were a whirlwind of Sheila recounting what had happened while Mr. Bloom grabbed towels from somewhere. Ben escorted Sheila to Courtney's car, annoyed that the cameraman followed along as if they were shooting a tightly directed episode of *CSI: Montana*.

Once Sheila was wrapped like a mummy and seated in the backseat, Ben grabbed Hank by the arm and pulled him off to the side.

"Tell me you didn't do it yet."

Hank gave a look of sheer frustration. "Every time I come close, either Ms. Newman or Mr. Bloom yells 'cut' and they talk between the two of them like we're not even there. I tell ya, this acting thing is harder than branding a bull."

"Good. You can't do it on camera. Sheila says it will be a disaster."

Hank stared blankly for two full seconds, and then relief spread across his face. "Well, that's just fine by me." He pushed back his hat by the brim. "I never did think this was a good idea."

He crossed over to the cars, where everyone had gathered. "I think that about does it. Come on, Andra. I'll take you back to work."

Courtney trundled over to Ben and threw her arms around him. "Sheila told me what you did." She stepped back, regarding him with an admiration he'd only ever seen in her eyes when she looked at their dad or Adam. "I apologize for everything I ever said about you."

"Thanks a lot." He chuckled as they started for the car. "Are you okay to drive?"

"I'm pregnant, not dead. Thanks for your concern, but it's not far and you have your rental car."

Ben noticed Sheila gazing at him through the car window with an actual genuine smile. He smiled back.

This time, she didn't look away.

Chapter 7

Sheila awoke the next morning with the sun streaming through the window in her room, reminding her that she'd been so dog-tired the night before that she hadn't even bothered to close the lacy curtains.

Dreamily, she sat up and stretched, feeling better than she'd felt in days. A sound night's sleep was one reason for her light mood. The other reason… Well… she wasn't entirely ready to admit to that yet.

Throwing back the covers, she remembered that today was D-day for the café. They didn't have to be there until noon, but she was pretty sure Courtney would want to get there a little early.

She leaped out of bed and grabbed her toiletry bag. As she eased out into the hallway, she couldn't help but glance down the hall at Ben's open door. He'd probably already gone downstairs to breakfast, but the thought of running into him didn't send her into a tizzy the way it had all week. What a relief.

She crossed the hall to the bathroom, and the sight of the old claw-foot tub made her smile. That hot shower last night after her unplanned water-park adventure had felt better than a week in a fancy spa. All her anxiety had eased out and she had emerged totally renewed.

Looking in the mirror, she paused. She should be mad at herself for falling into the creek and embarrassed for having to be rescued by the guy she'd been trying so hard to avoid all week. But somehow her predominant feeling was something her mom had always called "joyfulness."

A few minutes later, she was back in her room getting dressed in jeans and her peach lace peplum blouse—classy but casual, and perfect for TV. At the last second, she decided to wear her cross necklace again today. It couldn't hurt for a Christian to broadcast an expression of faith, however subtly, on national television. As she quickly made her bed, her eyes lit on the book on her bedside table. A sly smile blossomed again. Even in her exhausted state last night, she'd taken the time to read a couple of pages before drifting off.

She pulled the top of the bedspread over her pillows and grabbed the book. Since the invited customers would essentially be functioning as set dressing while the judges did their part today, there would surely be some hurry-up-and-wait time. She might as well be prepared.

She fetched her purse from the back of the desk chair where she'd flung it yesterday and was about to slip the book into it when the sight of her phone glaring up at her from its little compartment snapped her out of her dreamlike state. She hadn't even thought about checking her messages since yesterday afternoon shortly before her unexpected swim. After that the evening had been a blur of shivering, showering, eating hot soup, reenacting her story for the families with Ben and finally falling into bed—all coated with a covering of elated confusion.

Now, as reality trumped romantic illusion, she reached for the phone. She skimmed through a few inconsequential texts, then listened to her messages.

The first was marked Urgent. With a quivering voice, Karl announced that Claude wanted to take him golfing with Mr. Abbott, but he didn't know how to play golf. Sheila gave the phone a sideways glance. What did he expect from her? Some kind of verbal golf tutorial?

She tapped the return-call button and, much to her relief, got his voice mail. She gave a brief but encouraging pep talk, ending with, "You don't have to be Rory McIlroy. Just relax and you'll be great."

Clicking Send, she bit back a twinge of insecurity.

After answering a few more minor messages from work and an inquiry from her mom about Courtney, she released a sigh. Anxious to get downstairs, she took a step toward the door and started to put her phone away, then caught herself. *Kevin.* Why hadn't she even thought about checking in with him? With a slight groan, she wandered over to the window, reveling in the perfect spring morning as she clicked on his number in her contact list and put the phone to her ear.

"Good morning, beautiful." He sounded a little preoccupied, but pleased to hear from her. "How goes the trip? Did my surprise arrive yet?"

Relieved that he wasn't scolding her for not calling last night, she looked out at the yard below. A movement caught her eye, and she homed in on a big brown dog running from around the corner of the house. Pulling a leg under her, she sat on the window seat and leaned toward the glass, curious. "No. But I had a little bit of excitement yesterday."

"Oh, really?" There was a hint of distraction in his voice, as if he was trying to focus on her while doing something else.

The dog picked up what looked like a stick in its mouth and turned, tail wagging, to look back at something just out of her view. A moment later, someone appeared from around the corner of the house, and Sheila perked up. It was Ben.

Kevin continued. "Tell me about it."

As she started to relay the story, she watched Ben approach the dog, putting his hand out as if he expected the dog to give him the stick. "You should see this little ranch we went to yesterday. It's just beautiful."

Continuing on, she heard paper rustling and voices on Kevin's end of the line. He interjected an occasional "huh" or a puff of air to indicate that he was listening, but she had the distinct feeling that she didn't have his full attention. When she got to the part about dropping the shoe, she felt a little foolish. "I tried to fish it out of the creek and I fell in."

"You fell in?" The lack of amusement in his tone bordered on flat-out condescension. "Couldn't you just buy another pair of shoes?"

That wasn't exactly the point. Didn't he care that the water was freezing and she could have drowned? Or maybe she hadn't explained it very well. Somehow it had been a much more entertaining story when she and Ben had reenacted it in the parlor for his and Courtney's families.

Before she could respond, Kevin started speaking

again, but the muffled sound of his voice told her he was talking to someone there with him, not to her. While she waited, she looked out the window as Ben walked into the field to retrieve the stick he'd thrown. The dog seemed to be successfully training him.

Noticing that Kevin's end had gone silent again, she spoke. "Are you working?"

"Oh, yeah. No big. What were you saying?"

She decided to wrap it up quickly before making herself look like even more of a moron. "I got stuck in the middle of the creek and Courtney's brother, Ben, threw a lasso around me like I was a runaway horse. Isn't that funny?"

If it hadn't been for the ambient noise on his end, Sheila would have assumed her phone had died.

Finally, he spoke, but in a low, almost robotic tone. "I didn't know Courtney had a *brother.*" He paused, letting the weight of that last word sink like a stone. "What is he, like, married with three kids or something?"

"N-no." What an oddly random assumption. "He's not married."

"Does he live there? In Montana?"

"No, Courtney's not from here, remember? She's from Fresno."

"Oh. So her brother is visiting from Fresno." It came out sounding more like an accusation than a question.

"Yeah." She felt a need to shift the subject. "Her parents are here, too. They're just great. Her dad's a riot. You should see what he—"

"But you said you've mostly been spending time with the girls who own the café. What are their names?"

"Andra and Janessa. In fact, today's the day we—"

"Huh. I used to know a girl named Janessa." The confidence returned to Kevin's voice in a way that amplified her annoyance at his having just interrupted her. "She was a saleswoman in our division."

"Really?" She huffed out a tight-lipped response.

"Yeah. Come to think of it, her name was actually Jessica. Anyway, she used to…"

While Kevin told a story about some woman not named Janessa, Sheila folded her free arm across her middle and watched Ben engage in a new game with the dog that looked like a variation of tug-of-war. She smiled. This could entertain her all day, if she didn't have so much to do.

That thought jolted her, and she stood. "I really should go. I have to be at the café by noon."

"Oh. Right." He'd returned to his previous preoccupied demeanor. "Well, enjoy your day. Only nine more to go."

Her heart plummeted. She really didn't want to be reminded of how little time she had left here.

After clicking off, she watched Ben give up on the stick and pick up a rope instead. He started to twirl it around, finally swinging it and catching a fence post in the loop.

She suppressed a giggle. He looked a little clumsy and awkward, as if he wasn't used to roping, but he sure was cute.

The giggle turned to a groan. In spite of her best efforts not to fall for him, she had *literally* fallen, and he had managed to rope her in. She couldn't entirely trust him, but being around him seemed unavoidable.

Squaring her shoulders, she firmed her resolve. It might be okay to spend time around him, but she'd have to be more careful.

A little before noon, Sheila and Courtney arrived in town to find the street outside the café blocked off and looking like some kind of crazy media circus had come to town. The place was a sea of mysterious-looking trucks, trailers and tents, cables draped everywhere and people scurrying around wearing headsets and carrying coffee cups and clipboards.

At the door, the woman who had been there yesterday handing out forms checked their names against her list. Giving them succinct instructions to act natural for the camera and not to stare at the judges, she admitted them to what now looked more like a set for a show about the Golden Pear than the café itself. The place appeared to have been overrun not only by frenzied show staff but by media folks and customers who sat at their tables primping like movie extras. The sense of anticipation and buzz in the room indicated that the "party" wouldn't begin until the judges walked through the door.

At a table near the windows, Blair sat with a freshly preened Brian Leary, going over what looked like a script. Glancing around, Sheila saw no sign yet of Mr. Bloom, although she could tell Courtney was on the lookout.

Moving into the short line at the counter, Sheila cast an assessing look at her friend.

"Court, are you sure you want to be here? I mean, it could get a little stressful, don't you think?"

"Are you kidding? We've been waiting all week for this. I wouldn't miss it. Besides, I'm used to being on set, remember? It's what I do." She gazed confidently around the bustling space. "Adam's the one who needs to be home sleeping, which he is." She shook her head. "Thank goodness that last calf was born. Now things can get back to normal."

Suppressing a smirk, Sheila looked at Courtney's belly, wondering how long "normal" would last.

Placing both hands on her lower back, Courtney tilted a look at Sheila. "So those flowers Kevin sent sure are pretty."

"What? Oh. Yeah." It had come as somewhat of a relief that morning when Kevin's "surprise" had turned out to be a huge bouquet of pink-and-white roses and lilies. She hadn't realized how nervous she'd been that the promised gift might be something more serious, although a bouquet the size of a small tree seemed a bit disproportionate to the current status of their relationship.

Courtney studied the menu board, as if something new might have been added. "I guess Kevin doesn't know you very well yet."

Sheila jerked her head at her friend. "Why do you say that?"

Courtney raised her brows, letting a slight pause do some of the talking. "Just that any guy who knows you would know not to give you anything pink."

The words hit Sheila like a speeding Hollywood tour bus. Something about the flowers had needled at the back of her mind, but she'd been so busy trying to rally a sense of gratitude that she hadn't been able to pin it down. It was great that Kevin had sent flowers, but pink just wasn't her thing. She scolded herself. It wasn't fair of her to expect him to know that. They'd only met… What was it? Six, maybe seven weeks ago. How was he supposed to know she didn't like pink? Or that she wasn't really big on flowers. She'd prefer a nice bag of jelly beans any day.

They ordered salads and huckleberry lemonade, then claimed a table on the far side of a large one that had been set up importantly in the center of the room with four chairs on three of its sides. Empty space surrounded it like a moat, and a large sign sat in its center that read Reserved for Judges.

"The judges arrive at twelve-thirty, right?" Sheila checked her watch, wondering what was keeping Ben. "I hope your parents make it in time."

"Are you kidding? They wouldn't miss this."

Right on cue, Mr. and Mrs. Jacobs made their entrance along with Mrs. Greene, looking around like tourists at the Getty Center. Sheila held her breath, eyes glued to the door. A moment later, Ben walked up to the checklist woman, then entered the café. He immediately caught her eye and everything else in the room took on a surreal blur. She smiled, which won her a confident grin in return.

"This sure is exciting."

Sheila hadn't even realized that Courtney's parents had made their way across the room and were now standing next to them. Mrs. Greene had found Mr. Bloom, who had apparently slipped in without Sheila noticing. Courtney's eye kept ricocheting between him and Blair, who now moved about the room like a hostess checking on every last detail before the arrival of her guests.

As Mr. and Mrs. Jacobs sat at an adjacent table and Courtney twisted around in her chair to talk to them, Ben wound through the maze of tables and took the seat next to Sheila.

"Hey." An unprecedented shyness tightened her throat. "I just wanted to thank you again for… Well, you know. Reeling me in."

"My pleasure." A smile pulled at his lips. "Next week

Hank's teaching me ear tagging and branding, so unless you want your ears pierced again or a tattoo..."

Her hand shot up like a stop sign. "Thanks anyway, cowboy." Looking past Ben, she saw Hank enter and survey the room. "What's Hank going to do now that we put a damper on his plans?"

Letting out a slow breath, Ben shook his head. "I don't really know."

Hank removed his hat and hung it on a hook on the wall along with half a dozen others. Oddly enough, he carried another cowboy hat in his hands. He saw them and moved to join them.

Surprised to find herself not wanting to be rescued from being alone with Ben but instead feeling a bit disappointed, Sheila let out a breath.

Nodding a greeting, Hank took the remaining seat at their table and handed the hat to Ben.

Ben chuckled. "What's this?"

"I figured you've earned this, city boy."

Sheila couldn't help but giggle at the nickname. Ben put on the hat and affected a John Wayne swagger as best he could without standing up. "Thanks, pardner."

"My pleasure. You'll want to remember to remove that in the presence of a lady."

Looking at Sheila, Ben quickly removed it with a gentlemanly flourish, to which she responded with a prim ladylike nod.

"So," Ben ventured as he set the hat on his knee, "I'm guessing you didn't get a chance to talk to Andra last night."

Hank shook his head. "It just wasn't the right time. All she had on her mind was this show today, and rightly so."

"Well—" Sheila gave him what she hoped was an

encouraging look "—did you at least find out if she liked the ranch?"

"She loved it. Said it's exactly the kind of place where she'd like to live someday."

Ben and Sheila spoke over each other in encouragement.

Hank shook his head at their mutual show of hopefulness. "It doesn't matter now. The other guy I told you about put in his offer. I knew it would happen. It just wasn't meant to be, I guess."

"I'm really sorry to hear that," Sheila said.

"There'll be other places," Ben added.

Wishing she could do something to help, Sheila settled for a consoling pat on the arm as one of the servers delivered their salads. "I know how hard it is to want something you just can't get a grip on."

Ben looked away, and for a fleeting moment, she wondered if he was thinking the same thing she was. Had he wanted more with her? Did he want that now?

Hank gave her an appreciative look, then slapped his hands down on the table. "Hey, we're supposed to look like customers, right? I'm going to go order some lunch." He looked at Ben. "You want to come?"

A flash of reluctance crossed Ben's face that she wanted to attribute to a desire to stay with her, but he nodded and scooted back his chair.

As the boys headed toward the growing line at the counter, Courtney twisted back around. Her eyes widened at the sight of her salad.

"What were you guys talking to Hank about?"

Sheila considered how much she should tell her, deciding it was best to keep his proposal plans under wraps for now. "Just that someone else made an offer on that ranch."

"Oh. That's a shame." She watched the boys talking to each other as they stood in line. "I'm really glad the two of them hit it off. Hank's a good guy, and my brother doesn't have a lot of friends who aren't computer nerds."

Sheila chuckled. "It's funny. You keep calling him a nerd, but I just don't see him that way."

"No?" Courtney creased her brow. "How *do* you see him?"

Taking a sip of her lemonade to buy herself a moment, Sheila weighed her answer. "I think he's really funny and fun to be around." She allowed the sly smile that tugged at her lips. "And he's undeniably—"

"Ogle-worthy?" Courtney supplied with a girlish giggle.

Sheila joined in her mirth. "I know you can't see it, being his sister, but, yes. He's definitely ogle-worthy."

Courtney paused, her expression turning serious as she stabbed her fork into her salad. "You know, this is going to sound really strange." She allowed the bite of salad to hover over her plate. "But I had hoped you and Ben might get together."

Sheila's stomach did a flip that, if she'd been home in L.A., might have caused seismographic concern. "Oh…?"

"Yeah. I mean, he doesn't do much socializing, but he really hit it off with you last year. It seemed like you two were having fun together, so I thought…" She waved away the conclusion of her sentence. "Anyway, it doesn't matter."

An avalanche of emotions cascaded over Sheila, obscuring her thinking. If they'd had this conversation last summer, would things have gone differently? She struggled to find her voice. "Why didn't you say anything about this before?"

"I don't know." Swallowing, Courtney studied her salad. "I guess I didn't want you to feel pressured. Ben's a supersweet guy, but women just can't seem to get past his shyness. I know how great you are, and I just hoped..." Melancholy whitewashed her expression as she raked her fork through the plate of greens. "But I guess it doesn't matter now." She stabbed a hunk of lettuce and stuck it in her mouth, then chewed thoughtfully. After swallowing, she managed a small sincere-looking smile. "I really can't wait to meet Kevin."

Suddenly, Sheila felt an overwhelming need to know the truth about Stephanie. The Don Juan image she had in her head of Ben was so out of sync with the flesh-and-bone reality of him that she couldn't go another second without knowing.

She opened her mouth to speak just as Courtney's attention was diverted toward a flurry of activity over by the door. Sheila turned, too, as a man with shaggy hair and a Journey T-shirt instructed the two guys with cameras on their shoulders to position themselves by the door like sentries. All the crew members gravitated either to the door or out to the sidewalk. Through the window, Sheila could see the curtain of curious onlookers part for a small group of people who broke through and aimed for the entrance to the café.

A moment later, four very well-groomed people—two men and two women—entered, and an excited buzz filled the room. Sheila recognized them as an eminent cookbook author, the owner of a famous five-star Manhattan restaurant, a celebrated chef and the former host of a popular TV cooking show who was in the midst of reclaiming her career following a scandal.

As the buzz of their combined names filled the air, they made a practiced survey of the place and headed for the end of the line, which was conveniently short now that most of the people on the list had already arrived and ordered their food.

"Well," Courtney sighed, "I guess it's showtime."

By the time Sheila had recomposed a quick version of her Stephanie question, Hank and Ben were on their way back to the table carrying plates and drinks. The judges made their selections quickly, then worked their way to their table as a TV crew member swooped in to surreptitiously remove its sign.

Reminding herself not to stare as the judges claimed their seats, Sheila took a bite of her lunch. With her question about Ben's character wedged painfully in her throat, the last thing she wanted to do was eat, but it looked as though she wouldn't have another chance to talk to Courtney alone for quite some time.

The cameras were repositioned and as soon as their red lights flashed again, Brian Leary came out of the kitchen with Andra and Janessa, who looked professional in their crisp white chef jackets. He escorted them to the judges' table with the cameras catching their every move. In very dramatic fashion, he introduced the owners, then presented each of the four judges and their credentials. They all wore serious expressions more fitting of a jury ready to decide the fate of a couple of convicted killers than a group of pseudo celebs waiting to eat lunch, but Sheila assumed that was how they'd been directed. Still, it was a little daunting.

Courtney's face pinched, and she set her fork down, placing both hands on her belly.

Sheila's own stomach jolted. "Are you okay, Court?"

Courtney nodded. "Just another Braxton Hicks. I'm fine."

"Braxton what?" Ben practically dropped a half-eaten slice of crispbread pizza onto his plate.

Sheila guessed that he had even less experience with this kind of thing than she did, and they shared a look of alarm.

Courtney's pained expression eased, and she waved away their concern. "It's nothing to worry about. It's like a practice contraction."

Ben's brow creased with a combination of amusement, confusion and apprehension. "You need to practice?"

Her demeanor turned weary. "It's hard to explain. I'm fine, though."

Brian escorted the owners back to the kitchen, no doubt to give their final approval of the judges' order before releasing it for serving, and the judges carried on as if the cameras were invisible to them.

Sheila let her eyes meet Ben's and thought about her earlier conversation with Courtney. Had she shared her hopes for them becoming a couple with him, too? He gave her a little smile as he bit into his pizza, and her heart warmed.

Courtney's eyes darkened then, and Sheila followed her gaze to the table by the window where Mrs. Greene sat having lunch with Mr. Bloom. Blair had pulled up a chair and sat in the aisle alongside them. If she *was* vying to steal his affections away from Mrs. Greene, that had indeed been a blatant show of bravado.

Several minutes later, another round of whispers went up as Tawny and another café staff member came out of the kitchen, each carrying a tray with two plates. Looking a little wide-eyed, they walked through the café carrying their trays as if they held the royal jewels at a coronation.

There was a sense of forced small talk around the room as the cameras caught the reactions of the judges to their meal, and the rest of the diners tried not to watch them.

Sheila let her mind wander. Soon Courtney would have her baby, which would provide a much-needed distraction. Then both she and Ben would return to their respective homes and lives. Somehow the thought of going back to things the way they were when she left made her heart feel heavy. What was wrong with her?

After several minutes had passed, the shaggy-haired Journey fan called for a break and the camera operators relaxed. He instructed all the customers to put their forks down. "You can show a casual interest in the judging, but don't talk or move very much." He waved an arm as if he was used to giving this instruction and to it being obeyed without question. "Whatever you do, don't create a distraction."

Sheila flashed Courtney a "wow, he means business" look, and she returned a weak smile. She obediently set down her fork and rested her hands on her tummy.

Soon the director called for the cameras to roll again and tension hung thick in the air. Brian brought Andra and Janessa—sticking so close to each other it almost appeared as though the sleeves of their chef jackets had been sewn together—back out to face the judges.

Standing a few feet from the chairless side of the table, Andra and Janessa folded their hands in front of them. A hush fell over the café. This was the moment of truth.

Brian gave an overview of what each judge had ordered and invited the cookbook author, who looked considerably sterner than in the cheerful pictures on her book covers, to give her verdict.

Placing her elbows on the table, she laced her hands in front of herself as one of the cameramen zoomed in for a close-up. She slowly opened her mouth, drawing out the moment for as long as she reasonably could.

"I can sum up the experience of this croque-madame sandwich in one word. It was—"

"Ahhh…!"

Everyone in the room jerked their attention to Courtney, who had suddenly doubled over with both hands on her belly and had turned completely white.

Sheila put her hand on Courtney's shoulder, aware that people all around them were leaping to their feet. "What is it, Court? A contraction?"

"Call Adam." She barely got the words out through a raspy groan. "Tell him to meet us at the hospital."

Sheila grabbed her phone from her purse and fumbled to bring up Adam's number as Ben and their dad helped Courtney to her feet. Blair's voice carried above the suddenly talkative crowd, saying something about this being a first for their show.

Adrenaline coursed through Sheila's body as she relayed Courtney's message to a suddenly wide-awake Adam, then grabbed her purse and hurried to catch up with the Jacobs family.

She said a quick prayer as they all exited the café. Courtney had been wrong before. *This* was the real "showtime."

Chapter 8

Nervous excitement vibrated through the air in the hospital's birth-center family room. Sheila had been waiting there for hours with the Jacobs family, Mrs. Greene, Mr. Bloom and a procession of Thornton Springs residents. Janessa had arrived at some point along with Andra and Hank, beaming with the news that the judges had loved their food. They stood a really good chance of winning, but the importance of that had definitely been shoved to the back burner for the time being.

They really hadn't heard anything about how Courtney was doing other than that she was "progressing slowly," and that made Sheila uneasy. With each hour that passed, Courtney's words from earlier in the week, about there being a small chance that they might run into some complications, echoed a little louder in Sheila's head.

Now, as she sat in one of the too-hard seats, hearing

but not listening to soft background conversations, a talk show on the TV mounted in the corner and a few kids playing a game, Sheila stared at her shoes and said another little prayer.

She had a peripheral awareness of someone approaching her and glanced up to see Ben looking down at her with a faint attempt at a reassuring smile.

"Want to go get coffee?" The lightness of his tone did little to conceal his own nervousness, but she appreciated the effort.

With a silent nod, she stood.

After securing several promises that someone would call or find them the second anything happened, they took a little walk to find coffee and get some air. Not surprisingly, they wound up sitting on a bench on the third-floor courtyard—just the two of them and *The Great Gatsby.*

The stark hospital building rose up on three sides of the courtyard, but they faced the fourth side, which opened up to a railed-off view of the city of Helena. Since conversation would only lead them back to their concerns about the baby, Sheila took the book out of her bag and began reading aloud, picking up exactly where she and Ben had left off last summer. She remembered. And thought he might, too.

As she read, the smell of moist earth and primroses wafted from the waist-level planters at their backs, and the vague sound of a country song on someone's car radio serenaded them from the parking lot below.

After finishing a chapter and passing the book to Ben, Sheila realized that the city lights had started to pop on and the sky had softened from bright blue to a wash of sapphire, rose and violet. She glanced at her watch. Almost seven hours had passed since they had arrived at the hospital, but suddenly time was passing far too quickly.

She sat back, pulled her sweater around herself to fend off the chill in the air and looked out across the city as she enjoyed the soothing sound of Ben's voice.

After what seemed like just a couple of minutes, he elbowed her arm. "Chapter seven." He held the open book closer to her. "Your turn."

When she looked down, the black letters seemed to melt into gray paper, making them hard to decipher. "It's getting a little dark to read, don't you think?" She stretched her arms out in front of her. "We can always finish it inside."

"Sure...." Sticking the marker in place, he closed the book and looked out over the city. "But it's so nice out here. Let's not go in quite yet."

Contentment coated that idea and she settled back, enjoying the feeling of sitting almost close enough to touch but not quite. This was exactly what she'd hoped to avoid earlier in the week, but now instead of feeling like a fish on the end of a hook, she felt completely relaxed.

This was a day set apart from every other day, and she could just let cold harsh reality set back in tomorrow.

After a few moments, Ben broke the companionable silence. "It's weird—Courtney told me they wanted to wait to find out if they're having a boy or a girl."

"What's weird about that?"

"No, the weird part is that someone sent them an enormous bouquet of flowers. Did you see it?"

She caught her breath, not sure how to answer or if she even wanted to. "Flowers. Yes. They're pretty." *Profound, Sheila.* The thought of having to admit that the flowers were actually for her twisted her stomach into a slipknot.

"Yeah," Ben went on, "but they're so *pink.* I mean, what if it's a boy?"

She smiled. "Well, if it's a boy, we'll just have to hope that he's secure in his masculinity."

He laughed at that. "I guess he'll get over it. I mean, he'll be born to be a cowboy, right?"

"Or a cowgirl. He might be a she, you know."

"True. Anyway, those flowers were a nice gesture from whoever sent them. I guess it's the thought that counts." He jarred, as if he'd just remembered something. "Oh, speaking of gifts..."

He reached into the pocket of his jacket, and Sheila tweaked her head to see what he was up to.

He pulled out a small white bag and presented it to her.

"What's this?" Furrowing her brow, she took it, instantly knowing the answer to her own question.

Ben ran a hand behind his neck, suddenly seeming a little nervous. "I was in the candy store getting some jelly beans for myself and I thought maybe you hadn't had time to go in there yet, so I bought this for you."

She peered into the bag of colorful jewellike candies, and a laugh got caught up with the lump forming in her throat. "That was so sweet of you."

Relief colored his face.

With her mouth watering, she started to pick through the candy.

"Don't worry." Ben chuckled. "There aren't any pink ones."

Her head snapped up. "What? But...why...?"

He lifted a shoulder. "I just noticed you never buy

that color. And when I gave you the rest of mine last year, you ate all of them but the pink ones."

"You noticed that?"

"Yeah. You never wear pink, either."

A hot flush burned into her cheeks as a perfect example of the hue currently being discussed. "How did you know that? Did Courtney tell you?"

His brow furrowed at the question. "No, I just noticed. Even though I think it would look good on you." His gaze swept over her in a way that penetrated her soul. "It would look nice with your hair."

Absently, she combed her hand through the hair by her neck. "It would?"

"Uh-huh." He nodded, a nervous smile curving his lips. "I…uh…like your hair short, by the way."

She looked at him and broke into a nervous smile of her own. "Thanks." Holding the open bag out to him, she regarded the door that led back into the maternity wing, reminding herself that there was still a world beyond her and Ben and this peaceful urban courtyard.

Seeing that she was looking around, Ben popped some candy in his mouth and turned, too. "Hey." He stood. "I think I might see a way to keep us from having to go in just yet."

As he moved around to the other side of the planter that their bench backed up to, Sheila twisted in her seat to watch him. "What are you up to, city boy?"

He smiled. "You'll see in a minute."

Chewing on the candy, Sheila let her gaze wander. The hospital walls were all but obscured by several perfectly spaced trees that rose up from the planters. There were several benches but they hadn't seen another soul in all the time they'd been out here. This area was probably a kind of secret garden that went undiscovered by most hospital visitors. It felt special, like their own private sanctuary.

As Ben glanced up at the trees and then back at the walkway, Sheila heard her phone beep in her purse. Jolting at the thought that it was probably news about Courtney, she fumbled for the device and checked the screen. Relief mixed with disappointment when she saw Kevin's name.

Deciding to let his message go until later, she set the phone down on the bench, next to the book and the candy bag. She had let him know hours ago that she was at the hospital in Helena, but he hadn't responded. Admittedly, she was still a bit miffed about his reaction to her creek story and had little reason to give him a timely response.

"I wonder why no one else is out here," Ben mused as he knelt down on the other side of the center planters.

Glancing up at the top of his head, which was pretty much all she could see of him now, she frowned. What was he up to…?

Her phone persisted with a second beep, and she looked at it again, huffing out a vague annoyance at the sight of Kevin's name. She picked up the phone and did a quick read of the somewhat confusing messages, which seemed oddly demanding of her exact whereabouts. As off-putting as that was, she decided a crash course in boundary setting could wait. She tapped out a note about the pretty hospital courtyard, thinking he might appreciate her sharing some details of her day with him.

"Oh, perfect," Ben commented. "I see how it works."

Just as Sheila looked up to see what he was talking about, all the trees in the courtyard abruptly came alive with twinkling lights. She gasped. It was as if she'd been launched back in time to the wedding reception and they were once again in the backyard of the Bar-G.

Standing up behind the planter, Ben looked pleased. "Does this remind you of anything?"

She nodded. "A million stars." Unguarded thoughts raced through her mind as tears blurred her vision. Was he thinking the same thing? If she said any more, she knew her voice would betray her emotions, so all she could do was smile.

Slowly, he walked back around to where she sat. The latest song from the parking lot stopped and when a new one started, it was slow, perfect for the moment. He looked over his shoulder, to where the music was coming from, then turned back to her and lifted one corner of his mouth.

He held out a hand. "Would you like to dance?"

Her eyes met his and she felt the intensity of his gaze pass through her like a bolt of electricity. The force of it lifted her hand, and she allowed him to pull her to her feet. Before she knew it, his fingers were on her waist and hers were on his back and they were moving to the music.

She rested her head on his shoulder and closed her eyes. This was exactly what it had been like last summer, only somehow this felt even better.

As the song moved from the vocal to an instrumental section, he twirled her around and brought her back into his embrace like a wannabe Fred Astaire.

Surprised and impressed, she looked him in the eye and chuckled. "Your dancing has improved since last summer. Have you been practicing?"

"My dancing? Naw. I haven't had time with all the roping practice."

That brought a girlish giggle up from some deep part

of her she hadn't accessed in a very long time. "Well, if you enjoyed the reality-show experience, you're well on your way to being eligible to audition for *Dancing with the Cowboys.*"

"Let me guess." His voice sounded light and carefree. "Dancing and roping at the same time? I'll keep that in mind."

Her head gravitated back to his shoulder. "You already know how to reel in your partner."

That earned her a laugh. "I don't know, though. I think Hank was wrong."

"Wrong about what?"

"Well, I haven't tried to rope a cow yet, but I have a feeling that women are harder."

She smiled. "The thing is, you only have to rope one woman, provided you get the right one."

The silence coupled with a slight slowing of his feet made her wonder if she'd just crossed the borderline into flirtationland without getting her passport stamped.

Haltingly, he started to move his feet again. "How do I know if I've roped the right one?"

"I don't know." She shrugged, willing to step out on that limb. "If she doesn't run away."

His feet stopped again and he stepped back slightly, looking at her with a seriousness she hadn't seen before. "Sheila…"

Her stomach buckled. "What is it?"

He took a deep breath and another step back. "I've been trying all week to tell you something, and I just haven't found the right time. This might be the only chance I get."

Her heart started to gallop. She opened her mouth to tell him to go ahead, but the sound of the door opening jerked them apart. They both looked toward the door as the prominent form of a man appeared, silhouetted against the harsh fluorescent light of the inner hallway.

Sheila gasped. "Kevin."

Kevin's chest broadened even more than normal as he stood in the doorway gaping at them. He took a couple of slow strides forward, allowing the door to close behind him.

"Sheila." He held up his hands as if he might expect her to run into his arms. "Are you surprised to see me?"

"Uh…yes." Her heart fluttered inside her chest. *Surprised* didn't begin to cover it. "What are you doing here?"

Kevin stepped fully out into the courtyard, his product-perfect dark blond hair looking a little spikier than usual. "This morning when we talked, you seemed lonely, so I thought I'd surprise you."

"I seemed lonely?" She tried to recall the conversation. "What did I say that gave you that impression?"

"Maybe *lonely* isn't the right word. Bored?" He lifted his hands. "It doesn't matter."

His eyes fixed solidly on Ben as he took the final steps toward them and stuck out his hand. "I'm Sheila's boyfriend. Kevin Philips. And you are…?"

Sheila's stomach lurched. Had he really just christened himself as her boyfriend? Could he do that without her consent?

Ben looked at Kevin's outstretched hand for a moment before slowly extending his own. "I'm Ben Jacobs."

Pumping Ben's arm as if it were connected to a well, Kevin looked contemplative. "Right…." He released Ben's hand and addressed Sheila. "Isn't he the guy you said you met last year? The one who lives in Fresno?" Without allowing time for an answer, he spoke to Ben again. "I appreciate you looking out for my girl yesterday." He placed a firm arm around Sheila, pulling her toward him. "She told me about what happened. You rescuing her from that creek and everything." Squeezing her shoulder, Kevin gave her a kiss on the cheek.

Sheila wanted to pull away, her attraction to Kevin seeping out of her like water being drained from a tub.

Ben looked as if he couldn't quite keep up with what was happening. "It was—" he took a couple of steps toward the door, as if he wanted to bolt "—nice to meet you." Without so much as a glance at Sheila, he disappeared into the building.

Sheila stood there dumbfounded, feeling as if she'd just gotten the wind knocked out of her. As if Ben had just taken a piece of her with him, but the illogic of that made her head start to hurt.

Gripping her by both shoulders, Kevin turned her to face him. "Hey, I have a really great idea."

"What?" She lifted her hands to her chin, remembering what Ben had said about trying to say something to her all week. What was that all about?

"Why don't we check into catching an earlier flight home?"

"What?" She stared, then shook her head in disbelief. Surely she had misheard him. "Are you kidding?"

His face took on a look of defensive surprise. "No, I'm serious. We could be home by early morning, catch a few winks and take the day off together. See some of the sights in the city I've been wanting to show you."

Sights in the city? As in, *her own* city? "You want to leave right *now?* But..." She was at a loss. "That's ridiculous. Courtney is in labor, right now. She needs me."

"Sheila, look around." He did so himself, as if she might need that demonstrated. "This is a hospital. She has doctors and nurses. I'm sure she has family here, right? You and I are just in the way."

Sheila's mouth hung open, all thoughts and feelings held in suspension while she processed what he was saying.

"Look," he went on, "if it will make you feel any better, you can go on in there and say goodbye while I look up flight times." He pulled his phone out of his pocket and pushed the button to turn it on.

"Kevin—"

"I know." He kept his eyes fixed on the phone. "You'll need to go back and get your stuff. I'll be sure to allow time for that. We're, what, twenty minutes or so from that place where you were staying?"

She felt delirious. Her head started to spin. Calmly, she collected her thoughts and spoke. "I have never in my life met anybody who's as unbelievably narcissistic as you are."

He looked up from his phone, his expression flicking between amusement and outrage, as though he couldn't decide which one he actually felt. Letting out a breath, his face landed on a compromise of patient condescension. He put a hand on her arm. "Sheila—"

"I mean it." She pushed away his hand.

That lit a fire in his eyes. "You just need a minute to calm down."

"You have no idea what I need. You barely even know me."

"What is your problem?"

"What is my *problem?* Where do I start? My best friend is here in the hospital having a baby, which is the reason I came here, and you want me to just leave like you matter to me more than she does."

Shaking his head, he muttered, "You're unbelievable."

"*I'm* unbelievable? Really?"

He started tapping at his phone again. "I'm finding us a flight."

"Fine. Find a flight. The sooner, the better."

He looked at her and smiled, as if it pleased him that she was finally submitting to his will.

All she could think about was her unfinished conversation with Ben. And that even though she didn't understand quite how Stephanie figured into the situation, Ben was still a better man than Kevin by a country mile.

The elevator door opened on the first floor, and Ben shot out on legs that shook so much he could hardly walk straight. *A boyfriend.* He couldn't get it out of his head. Sheila had a boyfriend.

His Sheila.

He should have known. How could he have been so foolish to think that a girl as amazing as Sheila wouldn't already have somebody? Somebody more worthy than him.

The bland walls of the hallway blurred as he charged ahead, looking up just enough to avoid running headlong into a gurney being pushed by a guy in green scrubs. The antiseptic smell of the place and the faint sound of voices on an intercom calling out codes added to his sense of urgency to just get out of there.

Slowed by a man who was apparently just learning to operate the pair of crutches he wavered on unpredictably, Ben tried not to let loose with a guttural wail. If he could just get to his rental car, he'd be able to scream or hit the steering wheel or *something.* There had to be a way to process this onslaught of raw data without allowing it to break through to his heart.

At least he wasn't prone to drinking or any other

means of numbing himself from reality, because if he were, this would be impetus for a severely lost weekend. The only means of escapism he was vulnerable to were books and computers, but even those compulsions stayed too wholesome to register as vices.

What a loser. He couldn't even handle his heartache in a way worthy of writing a country song about.

That thought brought a fresh crushing blow to his chest as he remembered how it had felt to hold Sheila in his arms while they danced. That had been only a few minutes ago, but already it seemed as though a lifetime had passed.

Reaching the lobby, he darted around the man on crutches, set his sights on the wall of glass doors and moved resolutely ahead. Hurt rose up in him like smoke from a campfire.

I appreciate you looking out for my girl yesterday. The words made a direct hit to his heart. This guy knew about the creek incident. When had she told him? Sometime between when Ben had rescued her and held her in his arms and later on when they'd had so much fun acting it out for his family? When he'd been so naive to think they were getting back on track? Tears stung the backs of his eyes. At least he hadn't made a total fool of himself by telling her about the job transfer. *Yeah.* Or he could have moved and *then* found out about the bruiser with the iron grip. That would have been even worse.

He stepped onto the black mat in front of the doors, triggering them to slide open.

All he had to do was get as far away from here as possible. If that meant getting on a plane for Fresno tonight and staying there for the rest of his sad, single, solo life, then, great. That was what he would do.

Gaining on the parking garage, he took in a deep

breath. How was he supposed to get into the ranch house to grab his stuff if everyone who had a key was here? He sighed. He could have his parents pack up his stuff and bring it back with them. He worked his jaw. *Sure.* They'd be thrilled to do that for him after he'd abandoned them at the hospital without a ride back to the ranch. After he left without meeting his new niece or nephew or even knowing how his sister was. All because of a woman he was in love with and hadn't bothered to tell them about.

Great plan, genius.

Letting out a breath and shaking his head, he slowly turned around. His feet felt like lead as he started back toward the doors. *God, why? Why can't I just have this one thing?* And if he couldn't have Sheila, why did he have to stay there and watch her being happy with some guy who looked like David Beckham after he'd just missed a goal?

Kevin. The guy's name was Kevin.

As he reentered the hospital and trudged back across the lobby, he seriously considered calling his dad's cell phone and telling him he was sick and should stay downstairs, far away from anyone with a compromised or not-yet-developed immune system. Too bad he wasn't any good at lying.

At the place where the lobby opened into the long wide hallway, Ben paused, confused. He'd been blinded by his emotions just now on his way out and couldn't remember for the life of him which way the elevators were. The first time up he'd gotten directions, but a quick glance over his shoulder confirmed that there was no one now manning the front desk. Might as well just pick. Left looked promising, and if he didn't encounter the elevators fairly quickly, he'd just turn around and try the other way.

Slowing, he tried to convince himself that it wasn't so bad. Things were no worse than they'd been for him before he'd met Sheila. Last summer. When she'd probably had a boyfriend already.

Ugh. That thought hurt worse than getting shot in the head. Not that he'd ever actually gotten shot in the head, but he could imagine it would hurt.

Seeing the bank of elevators down the hall, he sighed. *Fine.* He'd go back upstairs and wait with his parents, then be happy for his sister. He hit the elevator button. He would wait till the baby was here and his parents were ready to go to the ranch. Then he would let them know he needed to leave tomorrow. Get back to work. That wouldn't be a lie, exactly, since that would be where he'd go. What else did he have to do, other than plan the rest of his dinner-for-one, single-bed, pathetic existence?

The elevator door opened and he waited for a patient in a wheelchair to be maneuvered out, then got in and punched the button for the third floor. As soon as the door shut, he closed his eyes. Sure, he would probably meet other women in his life, but it was hard to believe he could ever feel about anyone the way he felt about Sheila. There was a firewall around his heart that only she could disable. She was it, and he had blown it. But the worst part was that no matter how much he attempted to parse the situation, he couldn't even really know what he had done wrong.

If he had only said the right thing last summer, would things have gone differently?

Or...had she already had *Kevin* then?

He pinched his eyes closed even tighter as a pain he'd

never thought possible brewed in his chest. Had he just imagined that she'd felt something for him, too, even tonight when they were dancing?

The *ding* of the elevator jarred him out of that excruciating contemplation, and he opened his eyes. He really should be grateful. He'd been granted one more day's worth of sweet memories of Sheila. Wasn't that what he had asked for? He needed to be thankful for that, because it looked as if that was all he was going to get.

Stepping out of the elevator, he looked up, then stopped in his tracks. Nothing around him looked particularly familiar. At the place where he thought he remembered a nurse's station, there was a giant aquarium and a couple of chairs. Had he really been gone long enough for them to completely redecorate? He twisted around to check the large 3 above the elevator. This was the right floor, all right. *Great.* On top of everything else, he was now lost.

He started to walk, thinking that eventually he'd run into something that looked familiar or someone he could ask. Rounding a corner, he was pleased to see another nurse's station, bigger than the one they had passed on this floor earlier in the day.

"Excuse me." He stood in front of the counter where an older woman wearing green scrubs with blue-and-yellow cats on them sat with her eyes fixed to a computer screen.

The clacking of her keyboard ceased and she glanced up over her glasses. "Yes?"

"I'm lost." He gave a little chuckle, hoping to elicit some sympathy. "My sister's having a baby, and I went to the lobby and I guess I forgot to leave a trail of bread crumbs."

"You're in the wrong wing." Removing her glasses,

she nodded. "Happens all the time." She pointed back the way he'd come. "You want to go down the elevator you came up in to the first floor. Then go to the bank of elevators on the other side of the hallway leading off the main lobby."

Resisting the urge to comment on the inconvenience factor, he thanked her and turned to go.

"Or..."

He pivoted back around, his Lacava shoes squeaking on the spotless linoleum floor.

Using her glasses, she pointed past a snack machine to a hallway behind her. "You *could* take a shortcut through the courtyard. That'll take you right where you want to go if you don't mind being outside in the dark for a minute."

The courtyard? *Really?*

He smiled pleasantly. "Thanks anyway, but I think I'll go back downstairs."

"Suit yourself." She returned her glasses to her face. "I don't blame you, though. It's black as pitch out there."

He breathed out. "Not anymore."

"How's that?" She looked up.

"I just said it's not dark out there now." His voice sounded hollow in his ears, as if it were coming from somewhere down the hall. "A million stars are shining."

The look she gave him made him think she might just call someone from the psych ward to have him escorted from the building. He breathed out relief when all she did was shrug and return to her typing.

Thanking her again, he turned and headed back toward the elevators.

Suddenly, his steps slowed. He turned around, unable to pinpoint what it was that was niggling at the back of his mind, telling him to take her up on her suggestion.

His feet started to move toward that snack machine, and before he knew it, he was standing in front of a glass door exactly like the one opposite it over on the other side of the courtyard. The one that led to the maternity wing.

He peered through the glass. The trees were still sparkling like a convention of fireflies, but he didn't see anybody. Sheila and Kevin were probably inside by now, but even if they weren't, was he really in that much of a hurry?

He sighed. He was here for Courtney, and it wouldn't do anybody any good for him to waste more time. Besides, knowing his mom, she was probably ready to call hospital security to go track him down by now. He might as well buck up and take the shortcut.

He pulled open the door and stepped out into the night. Crisp air filled his lungs, reminding him of God's promise that as long as the earth lasts, there will always be cold and heat, day and night. There was an odd comfort in that as he started walking on the cement path between the planters.

A sound took him by surprise and he realized that someone was sitting on the bench where he and Sheila had sat reading a little while ago. Not wanting to disturb whoever it was, he quickened his steps, then stopped.

Crying. That was the sound. A gasping sort of sob.

His stomach leaped to his throat as he immediately thought of Courtney and the fact that he hadn't heard how things were going. No news was probably good news, but it could also mean that no one had thought to call him yet. He sidestepped around the edge of the planter just to make sure it was no one he knew.

It was Sheila, sitting with her back to him, bent over as if she was leaning on her arms, her shoulders shaking.

Oh, man. He was the worst brother in the world.

Something had gone terribly wrong, and he'd been so caught up in his own problems that he hadn't even…

"Sheila…?" Before he knew what he was doing, he was standing next to the bench, shaking in fear, wanting desperately to be wrong about the reason she was crying.

She jumped a little as she looked up. Her eyes were puffy and moist, and she clutched the book in front of her like a piece of armor.

Springing to her feet, she gasped as though she was struggling to get air. He froze, wanting to take her in his arms but resisting. His heart slammed against his ribs as he waited for her to tell him the news that obviously wasn't good.

Chapter 9

Ben was back. Standing right there in front of her. And all Sheila could do was clutch the book to her chest and sob like a baby.

"Sheila…what…?" Taking a step toward her, he held out a hand, then stopped just short of touching her arm. "Did something happen?"

Where was her voice? Biting her lower lip to keep from whimpering, she managed a nod. His face fell. Eyes darting around as though he thought he might see something lying on the ground that would help him know what to say, he ran a hand through his hair. Then with a slight shake of his head his eyes met hers again and he stepped forward, pulling her into a hug.

Surprised by that, she managed to get one arm around him while pressing the book firmly to her chest with the other.

When he stepped back, his eyes were glistening. "Tell me." His voice was barely a whisper.

Where was she supposed to start? She could see it now so clearly. She'd been clinging to the idea of Kevin out of desperation for a relationship, but he was the wrong man. Did the right man even exist outside of her own dreams? She looked at Ben—all flesh and bone and real and standing right in front of her. If only things could be different with him. If only she could trust him.

Composing her thoughts, she set the book down next to the bag of candy and sat. "I told Kevin to leave." She wiped a tear from her eye. "He just wasn't—"

"Wait a minute.... Kevin? This is about *Kevin?*" Taking the seat next to her, he let out a breathy "huh" and looked up to the night sky, his mouth curving into a grin.

She frowned. He was *laughing?* Hurt and confusion stepped aside for a tidal wave of righteous indignation. Her heart was broken and he was laughing.

"You mean—" he looked at her again "—the baby's okay?"

"What...?" Suddenly, she got it. He had assumed... She looked away, feeling like a fool for not understanding how this had seemed. She let out a breath. "Oh... yes, as far as I know."

His eyes closed, and she saw his lips move as if he was thanking God. When he opened them and looked at her, the urgency in his expression had dissipated. "Look." He rested his arm on the back of the bench and faced her. "I'm sorry. I just thought that..." He stopped as if the words were too terrible to say.

She held up a hand. "I know. I'm sorry. Everything's fine."

His eyes softened. "It's too bad about Kevin, though."

It was her turn to huff out a little laugh at her own out-of-control emotions. She shook her head. "I'm not really crying over Kevin." She folded her arms. "He didn't turn out to be the guy I thought he was."

"No?" A smile played on his lips as though that news somehow pleased him.

She couldn't help but smile back. "No. I just think that I've been so focused on my career that I haven't let myself have much of a personal life. I just wanted him to be the one."

He rolled in his lips and looked down, as if calculating the right response. "So how long were you two...?" He let that trail off, moving his index finger back and forth to indicate some sort of togetherness.

She startled. "Oh, no. We weren't..." She mimicked the gesture, wanting him to understand that they weren't ever a couple. "We only just met a few weeks ago, and we went out a few times. That whole 'boyfriend' label was his perspective, not mine."

She enjoyed the look of relief that washed over his boyish features, even if she was still mad at him. Why was she being so quick to assure him of her own virtue when she was so certain of his lacking the same quality?

She breathed out a sigh. "You were trying to tell me something earlier."

He glanced up. "Oh, right." He slapped his hands on his knees as though he was summoning his courage. "I have something I want to tell you, but I realize now that first there's something I have to ask you."

She bit the sides of her mouth. She couldn't allow herself to fall. She couldn't. No matter what he said.

Pulling in a deep breath, he looked her in the eye. "Our week together last summer meant the world to me."

Her heart jumped into her throat. She had to protect herself at all costs. She started to stand. "I don't—"

He grabbed hold of her wrist, pulling her down. "Please hear me out. Because a few minutes ago, I thought that something terrible had happened to my sister or her baby and that made everything that's standing in the way of really loving the people in my life seem not very important. Things like fear and pride. The way things have been going, I might not ever be brave enough again in my whole life to say this, so please stay and listen."

Her mouth froze around the verbal expression of all her own fear and pride, and she slowly shifted in her seat to give him her full attention.

He held up his hands as if he was at a loss. "I just don't understand what happened." He looked down, as though his shoes were fascinating. "I need you to explain why you suddenly dropped me the way you did."

Confusion and hurt rose up in her throat. "I dropped *you?*" Her head started to spin as if she were standing on one of those playground merry-go-rounds that threatened to steal her balance and send her flying. "What about *Stephanie?*"

"Stephanie?" He regarded her through narrowing eyes. "Who's Stephanie?"

So now he was going to try to lie about it? Or had that relationship really meant so little to him that he honestly couldn't remember? Her jaw firmed. "I heard you tell someone that your 'girlfriend, Stephanie,' was going to pick you up at the airport in Fresno."

He thought for a moment, and then his expression lightened and he burst out laughing.

She stared. He really thought this was funny?

He smiled as he spoke gently. "Stephanie is the four-year-old daughter of the couple who lives on the other side of my duplex. They volunteered to pick me up." He affected a confident air. "She's crazy about me."

Sheila couldn't speak beyond a weak "oh. . . ." Embarrassment washed over her along with the realization that she had spent almost a full year seething in jealousy over a preschooler. She put her face in her hands. "I'm so embarrassed."

"Now I get why you were so upset." He put a comforting hand on her arm. "But why didn't you just ask me?"

Good question. She lifted her eyes to meet his. "I guess I was embarrassed. I was hurt and angry and I didn't want you to know I'd overheard."

"I can't believe you thought I had a girlfriend. The truth is I haven't had a real girlfriend since...well... *ever.*"

"Really?" Relief mixed with joy, diluting her utter humiliation.

"Pathetic, right? The closest I've come to having a real girlfriend—besides Stephanie, I mean—was that week with you. Nobody else I've dated has been special enough for me to want to pursue anything. You can ask Courtney. She'll be happy to confirm what a total wallflower I am."

A laugh rumbled from her throat at the truth of that statement.

Taking her hand, he went on. "All I know is that the week we spent together was the best week of my life. If I had my way, I'd spend the rest of my days reading with you and going horseback riding and being together through all the hard times, too." He enclosed her hand in both of his. "Do you think that maybe we could hit Refresh and start over?"

She looked into his eyes, suddenly realizing that her initial impression of him, that he was a sweet, wonderful man, had been true. She'd made a snap judgment based on a misunderstanding and had been too full of pride to have a simple conversation with him that would have changed everything. She'd spent a year in misery as a result.

Her lips started to tremble and she could feel her eyes burning. "Ben. I think you're great. And as hard as a long-distance relationship might be, I—"

He held a finger in front of her lips. "I'm glad you mentioned that. Because the thing I've been trying to tell you all week is that I have an opportunity to move to L.A."

Her heart nearly stopped. Had she heard him right? All she could do was stare. "What?"

"My company has offered me a transfer if I want to take it."

The simultaneous *chime, buzz* of her phone and what she assumed to be his made them both jump, then laugh. She clutched at her purse while he reached into his pocket and they read at the same time.

"The baby's here!" she exclaimed, even though it was obvious that he'd also received Janessa's message.

"Kelli Anne Greene." Ben beamed. "I'm an uncle."

"Congratulations, Uncle Ben. And I'm a godmother."

He regarded her with a raised brow and half a goofy grin. "No kidding. Then you and I are going to be working together as a team because I happen to be Kelli's godfather."

"Well, what do you know?" Trying to quell the giddiness in her voice, she quickly tossed all her belongings into her purse and slung it over her shoulder. "I guess it's a good thing we get along so well."

"I guess it is." He offered his arm, and she slipped hers through it. Together they went back inside to meet the newest member of the family that wasn't yet hers—but hopefully someday would be.

An hour or so later, Ben sat in a really comfy chair in what looked more like a hotel room than a hospital birthing suite. Everything he had pictured involving a cold sterile space filled with beeping machines and harsh lighting had been totally unfounded. So, too, were the rules about two visitors at a time. Courtney looked as if she were hosting a party.

Across the room, Courtney sat propped up with pillows on a huge bed and holding an impossibly cute, tiny bundle of pink. Kelli had made the rounds and Ben had been surprised not only at how anxious he'd been to hold her but at how easy it had seemed. She'd opened those tiny blue eyes and he was sure she'd smiled at him. Favorite Uncle was a label he'd wear proudly, at least until Micah became legally qualified to contest it.

"This place is downright plush, Court." Sheila sat in a chair next to the bed, alternately cooing at the baby and sending Ben flirtatious glances. "How long do you get to stay here?"

"It *is* great, isn't it?" Courtney seemed more elated than exhausted. "But I'm anxious to get home. I think we'll try to leave tomorrow."

"And I'm sure Kelli's anxious to see her new room." Ben's mom sat next to his dad on a little couch by the window. "She's a lucky baby to have a Ben Jacobs original on her wall."

Ben swallowed hard as everyone turned to look at him.

Courtney frowned. "A *Ben* Jacobs original? Don't you mean…?" Her voice trailed off as she pointed at Dad.

Dad held up his hand. "I did the painting, but your brother did the design. It turns out my artistic talent has been passed down to the next generation."

Sheila gave Ben a surprised but impressed look.

He shrugged. "I guess my secret's out. I do more in my free time than write computer programs."

A soft ringing sound cut through the conversational commentary. Bobbing his head in apology, Hank reached into his pocket and silenced the sound, then said something to Andra and slipped out of the room.

"Well—" Mrs. Greene stood and moved over to the other side of the bed, where Adam sat with his arm around Courtney "—you know you'll have all the help you could want with this little one." Holding her hands folded in front of her, she looked as though she might burst into tears.

Adam smiled. "Mama, would you like to hold her again?"

Her arms shot out before he'd even finished the question. "Well, since you asked."

As Courtney handed over the baby, her eyes flew open wide. "Mama Greene! What is that?"

Taking Kelli, Mrs. Greene looked at her own hand. There was a collective movement around the room as people shifted to see what all the fuss was about. When Mrs. Greene turned, it became clear to Ben that she had something on her finger that was large enough for him to identify as a multicarat diamond.

"Mama!" Adam coughed out astonishment.

Janessa ran to her mother, double-checked the ring and gave her a hug, then did the same to Mr. Bloom, who was by now standing next to the woman Ben presumed to be the future Mrs. Bloom.

Courtney flapped her palms against the comforter she sat on. "But, Mama Greene, you said you didn't want to get married again."

Without taking her eyes off little Kelli, Mrs. Greene lifted her hand in a dismissive wave. "I only said that because I didn't think Travis did. Then, of course, I had to wonder when *Blair* came to town—"

"Blair?" Mr. Bloom frowned. "Don't tell me you were suspicious of Blair?"

"Me?" Mrs. Greene gave him that look women get when they've been doing too much thinking and not enough asking. "No…it's just that Courtney got me wondering…."

Everyone in the room looked at Courtney, who flashed an exaggerated look of innocence that she'd probably picked up from her years of working with diva movie actresses. "Hey, all I did was observe. Mr. B., I know that you and Blair are friends, but you *have* had your heads together an awful lot this past week."

Mr. Bloom laughed. "Blair and I have been talking about the delivery of this ring. She's the one who connected me with the jewelry designer, and we had a little concern about how and when it was being shipped."

Mrs. Greene gave Mr. Bloom the same loving look Ben had always liked seeing his own mom give to his dad. "I knew I could trust you, dear. Blair is a lovely woman, but I know your romantic interest in her was fleeting."

"A thing of the past." Mr. Bloom reached over to offer Kelli his finger.

Sheila giggled. "Boy, Court. I guess you're going to

have to retake that final exam if you want to get a passing grade in Matchmaking 101."

Courtney did the best she could to playfully kick her, sending her fuzzy pink bunny slipper sailing off the bed. Ben stood to go retrieve it for her.

"Besides," Mr. Bloom continued, "Blair's been asking my advice for months about a certain reality-show host. They've been keeping it quiet, but I think we'll be reading about them in the papers any day now."

A pleased murmur made its way around the collective group, and the conversation turned to wedding plans. As Ben put the bunny back on his sister's foot, he caught Sheila's eye and gave her a look that expressed all his hope for their future together. It would take some time and trial, but he was willing to follow his dad's example and humble himself to do whatever was necessary to become the husband God would have him be when the time came.

Kelli started to whimper and Ben looked over to see her face turning from peachy-pink to tomato-red under her little pink-and-blue-striped hat.

Adam reached over to reclaim her. "Well, folks. I think visiting time's about done."

While the group said their goodbyes and shifted toward the door, Ben waited for Sheila to give Courtney a hug.

"You know, Court—" Sheila stepped back "—you might have been wrong about Blair, but you *were* right about something."

Taking Kelli from Adam, Courtney made a teasing face at the baby. "About what?"

"You're busy now." Sheila affected a nonchalant shrug. "I'll tell you all about it later." She took Ben's arm and started for the door.

Flicking a glance over his shoulder, he wondered exactly what his sister had been right about. He smiled at the slack-jawed look she now wore and escorted Sheila out the door.

In the hallway, Andra stood next to an enthusiastic Hank, who was still on the phone.

"I'll get right back to you." He clicked off the call and gave them a look as if he were about to bust.

"Sweetie, what is it?" Andra tugged at his sleeve.

"That was my real estate agent, darlin'. He said that the other rancher withdrew his offer and he wants to know if I want him to submit mine." He gave her an entreating look. "So what do you think?"

Without missing a beat, Andra backhanded his upper arm. "What are you waiting for, cowboy? Call him back and say yes."

A big grin took over his face, and he threw his arms around her and twirled her around. Sheila squeezed Ben's arm and they both laughed.

"Just think." Andra got her footing as he set her back down. "Maybe someday you'll get around to asking me to marry you and we can live there together."

As they turned to go, Hank looked over his shoulder at Ben and gave him a thumbs-up. Ben just about laughed out loud as he watched his friend walk down the hall with his girl on his arm. He had to think that the good Lord had known that Ben would need a friend to spur him on this past week. It felt satisfying to think that maybe he had helped Hank, too.

Turning to Sheila, Ben took her hands in his. "I think I have a phone call to make, too."

"Oh, really?" She faked a playful innocence. "To whom?"

He smiled. "My boss."

"Oh, right." The corners of her mouth quivered as if she might be suppressing a smile. "And what are you going to say to him?"

"Hmm…I don't know." He looked at her as she lifted her chin and closed her eyes. He gave in to the urge to bend down and let his lips meet hers.

When they parted, he could barely speak above a whisper. "So what do you think? Should I call my boss and tell him yes?"

She smiled that sweet smile, the one he didn't want to live another day without seeing, then wrapped her arms around him. "What are you waiting for, cowboy?"

Chapter 10

The elevator door at Sheila's condominium opened and she and Ben glided out, fingers laced together and each pulling a rolling suitcase. As their eyes met, they shared the giddy smile that had led more than one person they'd encountered in Cancun to ask if they were on their honeymoon.

Of course, that hadn't been too hard to guess, considering that the water-park resort where they'd stayed specialized in honeymoon packages. It couldn't have been a more perfect week.

Now, as they walked down the hall toward the condo that had been Sheila's but now officially belonged to Mr. and Mrs. Ben Jacobs, Ben leaned over and gave her a spontaneous kiss. Caught off guard, she teetered on her Dior Escapade wedge sandals. Immediately, he dropped the handle to his suitcase and scooped her up in his arms.

With a shriek, she let go of her own suitcase and threw her arms around his broad shoulders. "What are you doing?" Breathless from giggling, she could scarcely get the words out.

"Well, considering the circumstances, Mrs. Jacobs, it shouldn't be too hard to figure out." He continued to walk the few feet to their door and stopped, realization creasing his brow.

Seeing his dilemma, she couldn't hold back a smirk. "Should have thought this one through a little better, huh?"

He stuck out his lip. "Things like this always look so easy in the movies."

"It's okay." Letting go with one arm, she eased her feet toward the floor. "You're allowed a second take."

He set her down, keeping his arm around her waist as he stuck his hand in his pocket and pulled out his keys. After unlocking the door, he pushed it open and moved to pick her up again, but she stopped him.

"Aren't you forgetting something else?"

Raising a questioning brow, he followed her eyes to their suitcases standing in the middle of the hallway like a couple of orphans.

He let out a little groan. "Okay, wait here."

She giggled as he retrieved the two bags, rolled them through the door and came back out into the hallway. He picked her up and gave her his signature grin, then kissed her as if he meant it. She relaxed in his arms. That kiss held all the promise of the vows they'd exchanged just a little over a week ago and made her heart sing with joy.

His eyes filled with tenderness as he maneuvered her through the door and actually managed to shut it with a well-placed kick.

She looked around their sunny condo, which looked even more cheerful now that it had his belongings filling in what she hadn't even realized were empty spaces. "Welcome home, husband."

"Thanks." He kissed her again.

She smiled. "You can put me down now if you want to."

"What if I *don't* want to?"

"Then your arms are going to get mighty sore."

"Hey, I've got roper's muscles now, remember?"

"Right. And I thought it was the racquetball court you went to every morning before work."

"Racquetball, rodeo." He set her down on the cocoa-colored leather sofa and held up his arms in a Popeye pose. "They're really not that different."

Laughing again, she reached over to grab his treasured Stetson from where he'd left it on the end table and flung it at him. "Sit down, cowboy."

He put the hat on and sat next to her, throwing his arm around her shoulders, then grabbed hold of her hand and kissed it.

Relaxing back into the sofa cushions, she glanced over at the coffee table, which was still brimming with the wedding gifts they'd opened the night before leaving for Cancun. "We have to find places for all these new things, you know."

"I know." He reached over to shove aside a box, pulling something out from underneath it. "Except this one. We need to put it to good use." He slipped the gift card from Karl out of its sleeve. "Couples golf lessons. I never thought I'd feel motivated to take up golf, but it's worth a try."

"Hey, it'll be fun." She flicked a hand across his

chest. "We can buy cute matching golf outfits so everyone will know we're together."

He chuckled. "At least I know they won't be pink."

"True. Besides, you might decide you like golf." She laughed. "And Karl will be happy to go with you anytime you want."

"If he has time. Mr. Hotshot Designer."

"True." Her heart warmed at the thought of Karl and how his confidence as a designer had skyrocketed since his promotion. Sheila missed working with him, but her new assistant, Allison, was a gem.

Besides, Sheila herself had received an unexpected promotion as a result of her appearance on *Food Fight.* The national exposure had brought Claude so many new clients that he needed a new partner. Sheila now had not only a larger office to go with her larger paycheck, but also more control over her schedule. What a blessing.

Leaning forward, Ben reached for another gift. "I know exactly where this should go." He held up the well-worn first edition of *The Great Gatsby.* "I think this should sit on the shelf over there, right above the desk. Where we can see it every day."

She smiled. "That was so nice of Mrs. Greene…oh, I mean Mrs. *Bloom,* to give it to us."

"Perfect wedding gift. Hey, speaking of gifts…" He stood, pumping his eyebrows like Groucho. "Wait here."

She scrambled to her feet as he moved across the room. "Hey, mister. Don't think you're the only one who remembered that we were arriving home on Valentine's Day."

While he disappeared into the bedroom, she scurried over to the desk. As she opened the drawer, she caught sight of the silver-embossed invitation they'd received from Andra and Hank just days before their own wedding. It sure was great to have an excuse to go back to Montana this summer. Not that she needed an excuse to visit her best friend-slash-sister-in-law, not to mention little Kelli. But it was always fun to attend a wedding. This would be her fourth trip to watch a Thornton Springs gal walk down the aisle. She smiled at the thought. There had to be something in the water in that place.

Plus, she was dying to see the Golden Pear now that the girls had used some of their *Food Fight* winnings to put the finishing touches on her original design.

She took the little white bag out of the drawer and shoved it quickly behind her back as Ben came out of the bedroom, also concealing something. Looking each other in the eye, they met in the middle of the room as though they were about to duel.

She craned her neck, pretending to try to see what he held behind his back, and he shifted to prevent it.

She sighed. "Okay. On three. One. Two. Three."

They each whipped out a small white bag and handed them to each other.

Ben looked pleased as he took his. "Don't think that valentines are easy to shop for when you're trying to avoid all things pink."

"Hey, you have it easy with me." She sifted through her bag. "Who needs chocolate and flowers when the world still has jelly beans?"

That won her a laugh. "I'm glad we're in agreement."

She watched as he fished around in his bag and took one out, then held it up to her mouth.

She gave it a discerning look. "Wait a minute, mister."

He examined it, somewhat defensively. "What?"

She angled him a look that said he shouldn't have to be told.

He looked at it again. "Hey, it's green."

"It's watermelon."

"It's *green.*" He twisted her a look. "And it's *red* on the inside, not pink."

"Close enough."

"Expand your horizons." He tried again to put it in her mouth.

She scurried away, darting to the other side of the coffee table. He ran after her, easily catching her and pulling her back down onto the sofa.

"I'll make a deal with you," she said, holding up a defensive hand. "I'll be adventurous and eat the watermelon if you'll promise to wear your cowboy hat when you're a groomsman in Hank's wedding."

"Deal." He put the candy in her mouth.

"Mmm." It was delicious. She grabbed his bag to search for another one. "What have I been missing all these years? Oh, you're going to look so cute standing up in church with your hat on."

"Well, thank you, ma'am. But in the interest of full disclosure, that was an easy deal to make. Hank already told me all the guys are wearing their hats in the wedding."

A little huff came out of her throat. "So it wasn't really a fair deal. Why didn't you tell me?"

He shrugged. "If you had asked me, I would have told you the truth. I'll always tell you the truth."

She smiled. The truth would set them free.

Unexpected tears of joy started to well up in her eyes, and she gave in to her urge to wrap herself around him. His arms felt warm and protective, and she didn't want to ever let go.

* * * * *

REQUEST YOUR FREE BOOKS!

2 FREE INSPIRATIONAL NOVELS PLUS 2 FREE MYSTERY GIFTS

Love Inspired™

YES! Please send me 2 FREE Love Inspired® novels and my 2 FREE mystery gifts (gifts are worth about $10). After receiving them, if I don't wish to receive any more books, I can return the shipping statement marked "cancel." If I don't cancel, I will receive 6 brand-new novels every month and be billed just $4.74 per book in the U.S. or $5.24 per book in Canada. That's a savings of at least 21% off the cover price. It's quite a bargain! Shipping and handling is just 50¢ per book in the U.S. and 75¢ per book in Canada.* I understand that accepting the 2 free books and gifts places me under no obligation to buy anything. I can always return a shipment and cancel at any time. Even if I never buy another book, the two free books and gifts are mine to keep forever.

105/305 IDN F49N

Name (PLEASE PRINT)

Address Apt. #

City State/Prov. Zip/Postal Code

Signature (if under 18, a parent or guardian must sign)

Mail to the **Harlequin® Reader Service:**
IN U.S.A.: P.O. Box 1867, Buffalo, NY 14240-1867
IN CANADA: P.O. Box 609, Fort Erie, Ontario L2A 5X3

Are you a subscriber to Love Inspired books and want to receive the larger-print edition?
Call 1-800-873-8635 or visit www.ReaderService.com.

* Terms and prices subject to change without notice. Prices do not include applicable taxes. Sales tax applicable in N.Y. Canadian residents will be charged applicable taxes. Offer not valid in Quebec. This offer is limited to one order per household. Not valid for current subscribers to Love Inspired books. All orders subject to credit approval. Credit or debit balances in a customer's account(s) may be offset by any other outstanding balance owed by or to the customer. Please allow 4 to 6 weeks for delivery. Offer available while quantities last.

Your Privacy—The Harlequin® Reader Service is committed to protecting your privacy. Our Privacy Policy is available online at www.ReaderService.com or upon request from the Harlequin Reader Service.
We make a portion of our mailing list available to reputable third parties that offer products we believe may interest you. If you prefer that we not exchange your name with third parties, or if you wish to clarify or modify your communication preferences, please visit us at www.ReaderService.com/consumerschoice or write to us at Harlequin Reader Service Preference Service, P.O. Box 9062, Buffalo, NY 14269. Include your complete name and address.

LIDIR13R

REQUEST YOUR FREE BOOKS!

2 FREE INSPIRATIONAL NOVELS PLUS 2 FREE MYSTERY GIFTS

Love Inspired HISTORICAL
INSPIRATIONAL HISTORICAL ROMANCE

YES! Please send me 2 FREE Love Inspired® Historical novels and my 2 FREE mystery gifts (gifts are worth about $10). After receiving them, if I don't wish to receive any more books, I can return the shipping statement marked "cancel." If I don't cancel, I will receive 4 brand-new novels every month and be billed just $4.74 per book in the U.S. or $5.24 per book in Canada. That's a savings of at least 21% off the cover price. It's quite a bargain! Shipping and handling is just 50¢ per book in the U.S. and 75¢ per book in Canada.* I understand that accepting the 2 free books and gifts places me under no obligation to buy anything. I can always return a shipment and cancel at any time. Even if I never buy another book, the two free books and gifts are mine to keep forever.

102/302 IDN F5CY

Name (PLEASE PRINT)

Address Apt. #

City State/Prov. Zip/Postal Code

Signature (if under 18, a parent or guardian must sign)

Mail to the **Harlequin® Reader Service:**
IN U.S.A.: P.O. Box 1867, Buffalo, NY 14240-1867
IN CANADA: P.O. Box 609, Fort Erie, Ontario L2A 5X3

Want to try two free books from another series?
Call 1-800-873-8635 or visit www.ReaderService.com.

* Terms and prices subject to change without notice. Prices do not include applicable taxes. Sales tax applicable in N.Y. Canadian residents will be charged applicable taxes. Offer not valid in Quebec. This offer is limited to one order per household. Not valid for current subscribers to Love Inspired Historical books. All orders subject to credit approval. Credit or debit balances in a customer's account(s) may be offset by any other outstanding balance owed by or to the customer. Please allow 4 to 6 weeks for delivery. Offer available while quantities last.

Your Privacy—The Harlequin® Reader Service is committed to protecting your privacy. Our Privacy Policy is available online at www.ReaderService.com or upon request from the Harlequin Reader Service.

We make a portion of our mailing list available to reputable third parties that offer products we believe may interest you. If you prefer that we not exchange your name with third parties, or if you wish to clarify or modify your communication preferences, please visit us at www.ReaderService.com/consumerschoice or write to us at Harlequin Reader Service Preference Service, P.O. Box 9062, Buffalo, NY 14269. Include your complete name and address.

LIHDIR13R

ReaderService.com

Manage your account online!

- Review your order history
- Manage your payments
- Update your address

We've designed the Harlequin® Reader Service website just for you.

Enjoy all the features!

- Reader excerpts from any series
- Respond to mailings and special monthly offers
- Discover new series available to you
- Browse the Bonus Bucks catalog
- Share your feedback

Visit us at:

ReaderService.com

RS13